"It's absolutely crazy, of course," she agreed breathlessly.

"Absolutely crazy," Ace agreed softly, his gray eyes darkening momentarily as she nervously moistened her dry lips with her tongue.

"However, before I completely lose all control of my senses, I think you'd better tell me to go away," he added thickly, his heart pounding like a sledgehammer as she responded to his light caress with a low moan. "Quite frankly—we're both likely to be in a whole lot of trouble, if I remain here any longer."

Dear Reader,

Welcome to the final book in our miniseries:

Everyone has special occasions in their life—times of celebration and excitement. Maybe it's a romantic event, an engagement or a wedding—or perhaps a wonderful family occasion, such as the birth of a baby. Or even a personal milestone—a thirtieth or fortieth birthday!

These are important times in our lives and in THE BIG EVENT! you can see how different couples react to these events. Whatever the occasion, romance and drama are guaranteed.

This month's book is the sassy and sensational **Baby Included!** by Mary Lyons. We hope you have enjoyed this series.

Happy reading!

The Editors

MARY LYONS

Baby Included!

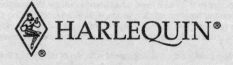

TORONTO • NEW YORK • LONDON
AMSTERDAM • PARIS • SYDNEY • HAMBURG
STOCKHOLM • ATHENS • TOKYO • MILAN • MADRID
PRAGUE • WARSAW • BUDAPEST • AUCKLAND

ISBN 0-373-11997-6

BABY INCLUDED!

First North American Publication 1998.

Copyright © 1998 by Mary Lyons.

CHAPTER ONE

'THE darkest hour is that before the dawn...'

As he recalled the old proverb, a grim smile flickered across the hard, tanned features of the man leaning casually against a pillar on the wide, shady veranda of his luxurious *casita.*

Well...at least it's a comforting thought, Ace told himself wryly. After the string of disasters which had recently been inflicted on his family he could certainly do with a bright 'new dawn'.

Fast approaching the watershed of his fortieth birthday, it seemed to Ace as if every single part of his life was now in the process of a dramatic change. Even as he stood here—sipping a long cold drink and gazing out at the dazzling snow-white beach of this exclusively private Philippine island resort—he knew there could be no escape from the many problems which awaited his return to Britain.

The younger son of a younger son, Ace had never— not even in his wildest dreams—imagined that he would one day find himself inheriting both his uncle Hector's title of Lord Ratcliffe and the large estate in the south of England. Which was why, as a very junior member of his family, he'd been able to choose his own path in life, first studying law at university, before going on to forge a successful career in the City of London.

Unfortunately, the past few years had proved to be disastrous, with one dreadful tragedy being quickly followed by another.

His own father's death, following a long, brave and

valiant fight against cancer, had not being entirely un-expected. However, the horrific car accident, mainly due to thick fog on the motorway, which had claimed the lives of his uncle Hector's son, wife and young family, had led to a profound and devastating series of events as far as Ace was concerned.

His uncle, Lord Ratcliffe, had never really recovered from the shock of losing his only son and heir. His death soon afterwards, following a massive stroke, had meant that Ace's much loved older brother, Mark, had inherited the title. But tragically he, too, had been killed in a com-pletely unforeseen accident while skiing in Switzerland, just under a month ago. And now Ace found himself the sole survivor of a family which had been virtually wiped out within the short space of two years.

Well…that wasn't strictly true, he reminded himself quickly. There was his own daughter, Emily.

He dearly loved the fourteen-year-old girl—at present living with his ex-wife, and going through a rather 'dif-ficult' stage of adolescence. Ace, with grim memories of his own misspent youth, was determined to be a helpful, understanding and supportive father. Maybe the recent family tragedies would help to bring them both closer together?

However, while anxious to improve his future rela-tionship with Emily, he was now going to have to take some immediate and far-reaching decisions about his in-heritance. Having lived and worked in London for most of his life, his current existence was a million light years away from ten thousand acres and the huge Palladian mansion currently referred to in the tourist guides as 'a classic example of a stately home'.

The people who write those books should try spending a night in the vast, crumbling old pile, Ace thought grimly. Because it had certainly never occurred to his uncle Hector—a tight-fisted, miserly old skinflint if ever there was one!—that he had both a duty and a responsibility to care for the large house on behalf of future generations of his family.

So, the net result was that Ratcliffe Hall was now a huge white elephant. Not only did it have a badly leaking roof—which let in more of the elements than it kept out—but also a mass of crumbling stonework and rotten timbers. Ace knew that it would need a fortune just to install some decent, modern plumbing—let alone try to do something about repairs to the basic structure.

Moreover, it wasn't just a case of bracing one's shoulders and facing up to personal tragedy. With each successive death he'd also found himself having to deal with the additional heavy burden of massive taxation.

As the senior partner of a large firm of lawyers, specialising in corporate tax and finance, he might well have the professional expertise to cope with the problem. But, following the tragic loss of his brother, Mark—only a few months after his inheriting the land and title from their uncle Hector—Ace had known that he would have little time to mourn. Not only had his brother left his affairs in a mess, but all too soon Ace knew that he was going to be faced with demands by the Inland Revenue, requiring payment of yet *another* large amount of death duties.

Although he, like everyone else in the land, hated having to pay taxes, Ace was certainly wealthy enough in his own right not to have a problem in finding the money. But exactly how he was going to deal with a large agricultural estate when he knew absolutely *nothing* about farming, he had no idea. In fact...

A slight movement at the corner of his eye distracted his gloomy thoughts for a moment. Turning his dark head, he watched a distant figure walking slowly across the white sand, before disappearing behind some palms at the far end of the beach.

'There she goes again—regular as clockwork,' he murmured to himself. Hardly needing to glance down at his watch, he knew that the stranger would be returning to her beach-side cottage, some hundred yards away from his own, in approximately one hour.

Did she spend her time sunbathing? Or merely sitting on the glistening white sand and gazing out at the ocean? Of course, there was always the possibility that she might be interested in exploring the coral reef. In which case...

'Oh, come on! *Grow up!*' he snapped irritably, his lips tight with exasperation at the thought of himself behaving in such a juvenile manner.

Following his attendance at an international tax conference in Manila, and desperately needing some peace and quiet in which to sort out his personal problems, Ace had decided to take a week's vacation. This remote island resort—only capable of being reached by private plane, and where guests were guaranteed total privacy—had sounded ideal. Which was why he was now so thoroughly annoyed with himself. It was clearly ridiculous—and a total waste of his valuable time—to be indulging in foolish, idle speculation about a fellow guest.

However, the facts were that he'd been at first intrigued and then increasingly curious as to why, in this scorching heat, anyone should feel it necessary to clothe themselves from head to toe in long flowing robes which completely concealed their figure. Nor could he understand why she wore such a very large, floppy hat, which effectively kept her face always hidden from view. Not exactly, in this day and age, the normal beach attire of a young woman.

Because, yes—mostly because of the wide-brimmed

hat—he was now quite certain that the distant figure *was* that of a woman. And from her sometimes quick, lively stride along the edge of the ocean he'd guessed that she must also be fairly young and agile. But why shroud herself in such a heavy disguise?

Amongst the many scenarios which had occurred to him, Ace had finally settled for the supposition that she might be someone famous, or in the public eye. But, if so, she certainly didn't seem to be typical of any prominent personalities he'd come across. Having been briefly married to a well-known model, it was his experience that such celebrities only thrived when fully exposed—and thus able to gain as much adulation and publicity as possible.

So, what mystery lay behind this woman's definitely unusual and baffling behaviour…?

'Forget it! It's none of your damn business,' he told himself roughly, putting down his empty glass and striding over to the desk, set in a shady corner of the wide veranda. Firmly banishing all thought of the strange woman, he sat down and began sorting through the large pile of papers in front of him, resolutely determined to concentrate on trying to sort out his late brother's tangled affairs.

Swimming slowly, just beneath the almost still surface of the ocean, Lois gazed down in wonder at the hidden world of the coral reef. Despite coming here as often as possible during her brief stay on this lovely island, she never ceased to marvel at the brilliant, iridescent colours of the tiny fish, darting and weaving their way through the long, pale knobbly fingers of the coral.

Although she'd spent the last few months travelling all over the globe, this enchanting subterranean world of pink and green sea anemones, and strangely coloured sea urchins, whose jelly-like fronds waved to and fro in the gentle ocean current, was certainly one of the highlights of her trip.

Having worked flat out for the last five years, Lois reckoned she'd been fully entitled to take a three-month vacation. It would, she reasoned, not only give her the opportunity of seeing some far-flung corners of the world, but would also be a good time to reassess her career. To think hard and long about what she wanted to do in the future.

From the moment when she'd gained a small role in *Ring of Destiny* right through to her last, Oscar-winning film, *Fear No Evil*, she'd hardly had time to draw breath—let alone take any time off to really consider where her career was heading.

Not that she was likely to face too many problems straight away. Winning an Oscar for Best Actress in her last film would certainly guarantee that she'd be offered just about any film she liked to star in when she returned to Hollywood. Playing 'feisty', modern heroines was all very well. But maybe it was about time that she extended her range by acting one of the more classical roles?

Oh, come on—who are you kidding? she asked herself roughly as she trod water for a moment, adjusting her snorkel. While the future direction of her career was very important, it was no good trying to pretend that it was the *sole* reason for taking such a long break from her work. Because, of course, the main impetus behind wanting to 'get away from it all' had been the urgent need to help cure her broken heart.

Unlike most of her fellow actresses, who seemed to have no problem flitting from one lover to another, Lois had finally forced herself to face the facts. She was, it seemed, one of those boring creatures: a nice, old-fashioned girl. Not that she was actively looking for a husband, she assured herself hurriedly. But one-night stands were definitely *not* her 'thing'. Which meant she'd found no problem turning down some of the well-known male Hollywood stars for whom 'commitment' was clearly a dirty word.

And that only goes to prove that pride comes before a fall! she told herself with disgust. Because what had she done? She'd just gone and fallen head over heels in love with a married man—*that* was what she'd done!

As the star of her last film, she might have been expected to fulfil that old Hollywood cliché and fall in love with her leading man. But, not her—oh, no! *She* had to be different, right? She had fallen hook, line and sinker for Ross Whitney—author of the best-selling novel *Fear No Evil* on which the film was based, who'd also written the screenplay.

It wasn't until they were halfway through shooting the film that she met Ross. He, as it turned out, actively hated the whole Hollywood scene, only agreeing to join the film crew on location to make necessary alterations to the script. So it was there, miles away from civilisation—and only too easy to forget the real world—that Lois had suddenly found herself fathoms deep in love with the tall, dark and diabolically handsome Englishman.

To be fair, Ross had behaved like a perfect gentleman. And that had been the trouble, of course. Maybe, given an ounce of encouragement, she might have cast her scruples to the wind and indulged in a really hot, scorching affair. Unfortunately, he'd kept her very firmly at arm's length.

In her own defence, it was fair to say that Lois hadn't known Ross Whitney was a married man. Well, not at first, anyway. And by the time she did find out it was far too late. In fact, when she'd gone completely over the top, and arrived uninvited at his privately owned Caribbean island, she had been in grave danger of making an absolute fool of herself.

Luckily, Ross and his estranged wife, Flora, had proved to be really nice people. And, of course, as soon as she'd sussed out the *real* situation, Lois had managed to find some hidden depths of pride and resolution. Just enough to enable her, however shakily, to retire from the field with her head held high.

In fact, she wasn't at all sure that it hadn't been her best performance: acting the part of a woman with clearly not a care in the world—and blithely wishing the two of them the very best of luck—before returning to the sanctuary of her own home and giving way to deep misery as she tried to mend her fragile, broken heart.

Still…no matter how hard she'd tried, and the many strict lectures she'd given herself, Lois had found it almost impossible to put Ross out of her mind—and her heart. Which was why this vacation had seemed such a very good idea. And, of course, that old proverb 'time is the best healer' had eventually proved to be true.

Somewhere…somehow, between viewing the Aztec ruins in Mexico and exploring the old city of Delhi, she'd managed to pull herself together. By the time she was recovering from a nasty dose of food poisoning— and being so kindly nursed back to health in that wonderfully luxurious hotel in Jaipur—Lois had woken up one morning to discover, to her complete astonishment, that she was no longer totally and irrevocably in love with Ross Whitney.

He would always have a special place in her heart, of course. But now she felt confident of being able to take that flight home to America tomorrow—quite safe in the knowledge that she was now ready to start a new life.

All the same…just make sure that in future you stay

well away from any tall, dark and ruthlessly attractive Englishmen! she warned herself grimly, before turning to swim slowly back to the shore.

'That's odd...' Ace muttered, frowning as he glanced down at his wristwatch. It was the first time, during the past four days, when the weirdly dressed woman had not kept to her rigid timetable.

Not that it was anything to do with him, of course. Absolutely *not*! In fact, it was definitely about time he learnt to mind his own business.

However, some ten minutes later he was still feeling slightly uneasy. He didn't want to make a nuisance of himself, of course. But perhaps it might be a good idea to take a stroll along the beach? Just to make sure that the woman really *was* all right...?

Rising from his seat behind the desk, he walked slowly down to the water's edge. And then, just as he was taking himself to task for being a fool, and about to return to his own *casita*, he heard a faint cry in the distance.

'Are you all right?' he called out some moments later as he ran swiftly towards the crumpled figure sitting hunched on the sand beside the ocean.

'No...I guess I've got myself into some...some sort of mess,' the woman replied, her American-accented voice sounding muffled beneath the hat and the voluminous gauzy outfit. She appeared to be concentrating on gripping hold of her foot with both hands.

It was only as he approached her and bent down that Ace was able to see blood seeping from between the fingers of the hands clasped so tightly about her ankle.

'Good Lord! What's happened?'

'I don't know how I could have been *such* an idiot.' The woman's voice was stronger now, and heavy with self-disgust. 'I didn't look where I was going. And I forgot just how sharp the coral can be.' She nodded towards the ocean, where the line of her footsteps, intermingled with some spots of blood, was clearly visible on the white sand.

'I think…well, I've got a horrid feeling that I may have cut into a vein, or something,' she continued with a slight wobble in her voice. 'Because, however hard I try, I can't seem to stop it bleeding.'

'There's no need to panic. Just try and stay calm,' Ace told her, swiftly assessing the situation. 'However, it's important to maintain pressure on the wound. So, keep holding on while I fix some bandages to tie around your ankle. OK?'

'OK.' She nodded. And then, as he quickly seized hold of some of the thin material swathed about her body, and began tearing it into strips, she cried, 'Hey— don't do that! I've got to keep out of the sun. Otherwise I'll burn to a crisp.'

'God preserve me from damn stupid women!' he muttered grimly. 'Do you want to get slightly burnt—or do you want to bleed to death?' he added, taking no notice of her protests as he carefully removed her fingers before binding the gauze 'bandages' tightly about her ankle.

'OK—OK…' she sighed. 'I guess I've been a bit of a fool. And I really ought to thank you for coming so promptly to my rescue.'

'That might not be a bad idea,' he agreed, with a sharp bark of sardonic laughter.

'I'm sure I'll be all right now,' she said as he rose to his feet, frowning anxiously down at his amateur handiwork, not at all sure how long it would hold the wound together.

'No. I think you're very far from "all right",' he told her firmly. 'You're going to need some professional help—and as soon as possible. Have you got a first aid kit in your bungalow?'

'I...I don't think so,' she muttered, burying her face in her bloodstained hands for a moment.

Ace's mouth tightened grimly. It was difficult to see anything under that damned hat. But, from what little he could see of her face, it was obvious that the woman's cheeks were deathly pale. Clearly there was no time to be lost in getting her some serious medical attention.

'Well, there's no point in hanging around here,' he told her firmly, before quickly bending down and scooping her up into his arms.

'Hey—what do you think you're doing?' she shrieked in a much stronger voice, the heavy voluminous garments hampering her movements as she tried to wriggle out of his grip. 'Put me down at once!'

Ignoring the frantic twisting and turning of the lightweight figure in his arms, Ace began striding rapidly back up the beach.

'I take it that you're not entirely stupid? So, don't you think it's time you started using your brain?' he demanded curtly.

When her only reply was a short, startled intake of breath, he continued grimly, 'That's only a temporary bandage which I've placed around your ankle. I don't expect it will hold the bleeding for very long. And especially not if you try to walk back up the beach to your bungalow. Got the message?'

'Oh, sure, I've got the message—you bully!' she retorted with a shaky laugh, before muttering something else under her breath.

'I'm sorry...I didn't quite catch what you said.'

'You weren't meant to!' she retorted. 'But if you *must* know I was reminding myself that I'd vowed to stay well away from tall, dark-haired Englishmen. And especially ones who are clearly hard, tough and *very* bossy!'

He glanced down at the girl in his arms. Somewhere along the line, possibly due to her frantic struggling, she seemed to have lost her wide-brimmed hat. However, it wasn't possible to tell the colour of her hair, since it was totally covered by a thick black scarf, knotted at the back of her head. Her face didn't look particularly appetising either—her bloodstained fingers having left ugly-looking russet-brown streaks across her pale cheeks and fore-head.

Only the wide blue eyes, heavily fringed by dark lashes, which appeared to be glinting with some emo-tion—although he wasn't quite sure whether it was anger or laughter—gave any hint that there might be a lot more to this woman than appeared obvious at the moment.

'Well, if it's any consolation,' Ace drawled as he mounted the steps to her veranda, 'I'm normally a *very* polite man. In fact, I wouldn't dream of being either "hard" or "bossy". Unless, of course, I find myself rescuing a grumpy American lady—who's clearly deter-mined not to listen to any of my good advice!' he added with a dry bark of sardonic laughter.

Striding swiftly into the cool, dim interior of the cot-tage, whose lay-out was similar to that of his own, he entered the bedroom and laid her gently down on the large four-poster bed.

'Oops! I guess that's put me well and truly in my place…huh?' She gave a heavy, almost theatrical sigh as she leaned back against the pillows. 'It must be really, *really* great to know that whatever happens in the big, bad world—*you* are always right.'

Staring grimly down at her, Ace had no problem in thinking of several crushing remarks which would put this irritating female very firmly in her place. And then, as he viewed the pale face, and slightly trembling hands, he realised that he'd been far too rough on this poor girl, who was now looking a lot younger than he'd at first supposed.

'I'm sorry. I should apologise for being so rude,' he said quietly. 'It's just that I was worried about the wound to your ankle. Believe me, you really *must* have it seen to by a doctor—and as soon as possible.'

'Yes, well...I guess it's my turn to apologise. I've obviously been a real pain in the neck,' she admitted, gazing up in some bewilderment at the deeply tanned, hawk-like features of the tall, dark and remarkably handsome man who'd just rescued her from a nasty predicament.

'I...I can't think what's come over me,' she continued in a slightly weak, breathless tone of voice. 'Because, I don't...I *really* don't usually behave like this.'

'I'm sure you don't. And—although you may find it difficult to believe—neither do I!' He grinned. 'So, I'm just going to ring through to the main hotel and ask them to provide some medical assistance. Once I'm satisfied that help is on the way, I promise to leave you well alone. OK?'

'No...no...please don't go,' she begged, swiftly reaching up to catch hold of his hand. 'Not...well, not until after I've seen the doctor.'

'Relax—there's no need to worry. I'll definitely stay here for as long as you need me,' he promised, before leaving the room.

Goodness knows what it was about this highly disturbing girl... Ace mused as he lifted the phone to call the main hotel. She looked a complete mess, of course. But there was something about the tone of her voice— and the soft gleam in those startling blue eyes—which was clearly having a rather odd effect on him. In fact,

ridiculous as it might seem, he was definitely beginning
to find her sexually attractive!

Luckily the hotel was able to arrange immediate attention. And Ace, waiting out on the veranda, was relieved when the doctor confirmed that the patient was
now well out of danger.

'You did well to stop the bleeding in time,' the elderly
stout man puffed, brandishing a large white handkerchief
as he wiped the perspiration from his brow. 'However,
the cut is not too serious. Provided that you look after
your wife, and make sure that she stays in bed for the
rest of the day, she will be quite well enough to fly back
to America tomorrow.'

'What...?' Ace gazed at him in astonishment. 'I'm
sorry...you clearly don't understand the situation. I can
assure you that this lady is very definitely *not* my wife.
In fact...'

'Ah, yes, I see how it is—you lucky dog!' the doctor
chuckled, giving the Englishman a sharp dig in the ribs.
'We are, of course, both men of the world. So, there is
no need to worry. Your secret is quite safe with me,' he
added, with a friendly slap on the tall man's shoulders,
before making his way back down the steps of the veranda. 'I will leave you to look after the lovely "lady",
yes?'

'No! I mean...you've got hold of the wrong end of
the stick!' he called out as the doctor disappeared from
sight, leaving only the sound of a hoarse, rumbling laugh
hanging heavily in the air behind him.

Ace brushed a hand roughly through his dark hair.
What in the hell was he supposed to do now?

The idea of being forced to look after that strange,
weird-looking girl was hardly a tempting prospect. All
the same...he could hardly walk away and leave her on
her own. However, with any luck she would by now be

feeling tired, and only too pleased to see the back of
him. Right?

Definitely feeling in need of a stiff drink, Ace braced
his shoulders and forced himself to knock on the bedroom door.

'I'm sorry to have to say that the doctor, for some
strange reason, seems to have completely the wrong idea
about us,' he said as he entered the room. 'While I'm
quite willing to do what I can, I really don't think—
Good God!'

Making his way slowly across the large room, Ace—
feeling as though he'd been hit on the head by a heavy
lead pipe—was having considerable difficulty in accept-
ing the evidence of his own eyes. What on earth had
happened to the blood-streaked, almost grubby-looking
figure of the woman whom he'd rescued from the beach
less than an hour ago...?

'I simply *don't* believe it!' he breathed, his stunned
gaze travelling up over the long shapely legs and lightly
tanned, hourglass figure, tantalisingly covered by a di-
aphanous chiffon wrap over a minuscule blue bikini
which left virtually *nothing* to the imagination. In place
of that hideous black scarf there was now a mane of
long, wavy red hair—like a fiery, brilliant sunburst on
the pillow—surrounding a perfect heart-shaped face,
enormously wide blue eyes, and a mouth which curved
as sensually as her firm, full breasts.

'I must have died—and gone straight to heaven!' he
exclaimed huskily. 'Because you have to be *the* most
utterly gorgeous...fantastically beautiful girl I've *ever*
seen!'

And then, as she gave a peal of laughter at the sound
of his hoarse, strangled voice, and his stunned expression, he clutched hold of one of the bedposts and made
a determined effort to clear his mind.

'I…er…I'm sorry,' he muttered, his cheeks flushing slightly as he realised that he'd been behaving like a stupid idiot. 'It's just that…' He gave a distracted shake of his dark head, completely unable to put into words the effect she was having on his normally well-controlled self.

'Hey—relax! There's no need to apologise,' the girl assured him. 'I don't know why the British have a reputation for being so formal and icily polite,' she added, with a surprisingly breathless shaky laugh. 'In my experience, you guys seem to be born with an amazing ability to make a girl feel like a million dollars!'

'I wish it was true. But I fear you're sadly mistaken.' Ace smiled ruefully down at the beautiful creature lying so elegantly stretched out on the bed. 'Unfortunately, most of the time we look—and act—as if we're well and truly strangled by our old school ties!'

'Oh, really…?' She grinned. 'Well, since you clearly *aren't* wearing a tie at the moment, how about fixing us both something to drink?'

'If the doctor gave you any medicine, you ought to avoid alcohol,' he warned.

'It's OK. I haven't even taken any aspirins,' she assured him. 'Although I normally drink very little, I reckon that after today's misadventures I could do with a stiff dose of brandy.'

'That sounds like an extremely good idea,' he agreed, grateful for the opportunity, however brief, in which to make a determined effort to pull himself together.

It was clearly ridiculous for a grown man, approaching forty years of age, to find himself so completely bowled over by a girl—however lovely she might be, he told himself, his lips tightening grimly as he mixed their drinks at the bar in the large sitting room.

After all, following the break-up of his marriage, he'd

had plenty of glamorous, highly attractive girlfriends, *none* of whom had caused him to lose a wink of sleep at night, or produced even the slightest ripple in his life. So why…why should it take just one brief smile from that admittedly beautiful but troublesome American girl…and he was straight into meltdown?

In fact, if he didn't get his act together—and fast!— he was going to be in dead trouble, Ace warned himself sternly. So, he'd better get the hell out of here, and as soon as possible.

'Well, now…' he drawled some minutes later, sipping his brandy as he leaned casually against one of the tall, wooden posts at the end of the bed. 'I'm hoping you can solve the mystery of why, for the past few days, you've been dressed like an old bag lady? Why cover yourself from head to toe in thick layers of gauze? Not to mention the reason for wearing that quite dreadful hat!'

'There's no mystery. I was just being very careful not to get sunburned.' The ravishingly lovely girl grinned up at him, before holding up a lock of her fiery red hair. 'Unfortunately, with my kind of skin, if I sit in the sun for even ten minutes I turn a bright shade of lobster. And if you want to spend some time in the water, wearing total block isn't always the answer, either.'

'But you've got a wonderful tan,' he protested, attempting to keep his gaze well away from her luscious figure.

She shrugged. 'Well, I'm sorry to have to tell you that like everything else in show business it's false. Just an illusion.'

'I know nothing about ''show business'', as you call it.' Ace shrugged, before walking through into the other room to fix them both another drink. 'In fact, I can't recall the last time I went to see a play or a film. And

I'm not exactly keen on the ballet, either,' he added,
returning to place a glass in her hand.

'Oh, Lord…!' he continued, his hooded grey eyes
gleaming with amusement as he stood looking down at
her. 'I hope I haven't said the wrong thing? Are you a
dancer?'

'No, I most certainly am not!' she laughed. 'Anyway,
who cares about what either of us does for a living? I'm
far more interested in the fact that I don't even know
your name.'

'Yes, I suppose we ought to introduce ourselves.
So…'

'Just a minute.' She winced, struggling to adjust the
pillows behind her head. 'I seem to be getting a real
crick in my neck, staring up at you like this. How about
taking the weight off your feet?' she added, patting the
bed beside her.

Maybe it had been a great mistake to pour them both
a second drink. Because, when thinking about the episode, much later, Ace would totally fail to understand
why he'd chosen to ignore the loud warning bells ringing
so urgently in his head as he slowly lowered himself
down onto the soft mattress.

'That's much better,' she sighed, raising a hand to rub
the back of her neck. 'So, how about if I kick off by
saying that, as far as Christian names are concerned, my
parents chose to call me Eloise.'

'Well, Eloise…' he began, suddenly uncomfortably
aware of the effect that the close proximity of this amazingly sexy girl was having on his body. 'I…er…I regret
to have to tell you that I am one of those *very* boring
members of society—a lawyer. And, even worse, at *my*
christening I was burdened with the truly awful names
of Algernon Cedric Emerson!'

'I'm not sure that ''awful'' is exactly the right word,'

she murmured, clearly trying not to laugh. 'I'd be more inclined to call it downright cruel. Because I'm afraid that there is nothing in the least romantic about the name Algernon.'

'You're so right!' he drawled, desperately fighting a totally crazy, insane urge to make mad, passionate love to this gorgeous creature who was smiling so enchantingly up at him. 'Which is why, from my earliest years, I've insisted on being called by the name formed by my initials.'

'Hmm...that's a lot better,' she agreed, the warm gleam in her wide blue eyes causing his pulse to begin racing out of control. 'Yes, I think that Ace is just about the perfect name for a guy like you.'

There was a long silence as they gazed at one another, the smile slowly dying from her lips, her cheeks reddening slightly under his steady gaze.

'I could be very wrong, of course,' he said slowly, 'but I have the distinct impression that there's definitely something going on here, between the two of us?'

'Well...er...maybe...yes. I think you could possibly be right,' she agreed breathlessly. 'It's absolutely crazy, of course.'

'Absolutely crazy,' he agreed softly, his grey eyes darkening momentarily as she nervously moistened her dry lips with her tongue.

'And...and we hardly know one another,' she added with a helpless shrug, closing her eyes for a moment as a deep crimson flush spread over her face. 'But...well, the truth is...um...I have to confess that I'm certainly feeling very...er...very peculiar!'

'Believe me—you're not the only one!' he murmured huskily. Raising a hand, he brushed a stray tendril of hair from her brow before gently trailing his fingers over her cheeks and on down over the incredibly soft, velvety

flesh of her neck to the creamy hollows at the base of
her throat.

'However, before I completely lose all control of my
senses, I think you'd better tell me to go away,' he added
thickly, his heart pounding like a sledgehammer as she
responded to his light caress with a low moan. 'Quite
frankly—we're both likely to be in a whole lot of trouble
if I remain here any longer.'

'No...don't go,' she whispered softly, raising her
arms and placing them about his dark head, before drawing him slowly down towards her. 'I really don't understand what's happening to me. And...and I can promise
you that I've *never* done anything like this before. But
please...please don't go.'

'Wild horses wouldn't be able to drag me away!' he
breathed huskily, before gathering the slim figure up into
his arms, his mouth closing possessively over her soft,
trembling lips.

CHAPTER TWO

ACE put down his pen, sighing heavily as he leaned back in his chair and gazed out through the window of his study at the trees and parkland surrounding Ratcliffe Hall.

It was now three months since he'd returned from abroad. A hard, frantically busy three months, dealing with the burdensome legacy of his inheritance: a dilapidated 'stately home' and an estate which had been badly neglected for many years.

With so much work to do—including many long, drawn-out meetings with the family trustees—he'd had no alternative but to resign from his position as senior partner of the large firm of lawyers in London. However, while he'd originally thought that he might miss the cut and thrust of City business, Ace had been surprised to discover that he'd gained a considerable bonus. Despite now being forced by circumstances to live in the country, he'd found himself actively enjoying the slower pace of quiet, rural life. But that was just about the *only* silver lining to the dark clouds which still loomed over his unexpected inheritance.

His young daughter, Emily, appeared to find the whole situation highly amusing—'It's really cool, Dad— totally far out!' But Ace wasn't particularly thrilled about the fact that, following so many close relatives' deaths, he'd now inherited a title first granted to his family by Henry VIII.

As he had told one of his oldest friends the other day, 'Quite frankly, to be now known and addressed as Lord

Ratcliffe has to be a complete anachronism in this day and age. Of course, it's quite useful if I want to book a table in a restaurant,' he'd added with a wry smile. 'But in all other respects it seems a bit pointless.'

Ace was, in fact, far more concerned with the many important, vital decisions he would have to take concerning the large estate, amounting to some ten thousand acres.

After calling in agricultural experts, he had learned that, while the land itself was in good heart, the various farmhouses, farm buildings, machinery and livestock had been badly neglected. Unlike his uncle Hector, who'd successfully managed to ignore the problem for so many years, Ace felt it was both his duty and responsibility to do everything he could on behalf of the people and the families living on his estate. Unfortunately, there was also the serious problem of exactly *what* he was going to do about Ratcliffe Hall.

Pushing back his chair and rising to his feet, he began to prowl restlessly around the large room.

Having made enquiries, he was now in no doubt that, as matters stood at present, it was useless to even think of trying to sell the huge old mansion. No one with any sense would dream of taking on such a massive house. Especially one which needed a great deal of money to be spent on its restoration.

And that was proving to be a real problem. It wasn't that he couldn't afford to pay for the repairs—having worked so hard in the City for the last twenty years, he was now very wealthy in his own right—but, as his own financial advisers had pointed out, why would a divorced man, with no intention of remarrying in the foreseeable future, want to spend a fortune restoring such a huge building which was clearly designed for a large family?

In fact, the whole problem of what to do about

Ratcliffe Hall had proved to be nothing but a major headache. Until he'd heard about the needs of film and television companies, who were continually searching for large old houses in which to film their various productions. Which was why, after he'd swiftly contacted several agencies, he'd been pleased to have a TV crew here last month, filming the exterior of the Hall for an Edwardian-style version of Shakespeare's *Comedy of Errors*.

It wasn't the complete answer, of course. Although the fee which he'd received for the use of the place was almost indecently large, it was a mere drop in the ocean as far as paying for any serious repairs was concerned. Still, it was a start. And with the arrival yesterday of an American-financed film company, prepared to take over and use the whole of the mansion for at least a month, it now looked as though he could stop worrying about the house. For the time being, at least.

He'd also been successful in persuading the tax authorities to take, in part-settlement of death duties, two huge Old Master paintings. While they had been all that was left of a once large, well-known collection, he wasn't prepared to spend too long regretting their departure. Especially since the dark, gloomy scenes of religious life had been highly depressing.

So, all in all, he hadn't done too badly over these last three months, Ace assured himself. In fact...

His thoughts interrupted by the shrill, ringing tones of the telephone, he strode back to his desk and lifted the receiver.

Grimacing at the all too familiar sounds of his ex-wife's breathless, child-like voice, he waited with grim patience to discover what she wanted. Because, of course, Martina wouldn't dream of ringing him up—not unless she needed something. He could only hope that there was no problem with his daughter, Emily.

Looking back, it seemed to Ace as if their marriage had been doomed from the start. Originally captivated by the tall, exquisitely beautiful model, whose face had adorned so many magazine covers, it hadn't been long before he'd discovered that there was very little in that lovely blonde head. And, to be fair, she had obviously been disappointed to find that she'd married a man who not only took his work seriously, but whom she clearly regarded as a boring workaholic.

Missing the world of the media and show business, it hadn't been long before Martina had run away from home to live with a cockney pop star. She had also taken their small young daughter with her. Despite desperately missing his little girl, and being prepared to do just about anything to ensure his daughter's happiness, Ace had bent over backwards to ensure that he remained on good, friendly terms with both his ex-wife and the new man in her life, Joe Tucker.

Surprisingly, it hadn't proved to be too hard a task. The pop star had turned out to be a basically kind and thoroughly decent man. And Ace could only admire the fact that Joe—professionally known as Frank N. Stein, and lead singer of the Raving Monsters—had turned out to be far too shrewd and down-to-earth to make the mistake of marrying Martina.

Unfortunately, as time had gone by, it began to seem that neither the pop star or Ace's ex-wife had any idea of how to cope with Emily, by now a thoroughly difficult fourteen-year-old adolescent. And Ace himself was also becoming increasingly worried about the young girl— not only going through a typically 'rebellious' phase of life, but also receiving little discipline from her butterfly-minded mother.

'OK…OK…' he sighed, cutting across his ex-wife's ramblings. 'I've got the picture. And you can tell Emily that I'm *thoroughly* ashamed of her behaviour. What on earth possessed her to swear at her teacher? There's absolutely *no* excuse for such bad manners. Quite frankly, she's very lucky to find herself suspended from school for only a few weeks,' he added grimly. 'Yes…yes, of course…if you're having to go abroad for a few days she's more than welcome to stay here with me. In fact, she can probably make herself useful by keeping the film company off my back.'

And that last remark, he told himself ruefully, putting down the phone some minutes later, had been a *bad* mistake. Because as soon as his ex-wife had heard the magic words 'film company' he'd had the greatest difficulty in persuading her that while Emily was more than welcome Martina definitely was not.

On top of which, there had been a decidedly unwelcome over-friendly tone in his ex-wife's voice. In fact, he told himself with a frown, if it didn't sound *too* ridiculous, it had almost seemed as if she'd been seeking some form of reconciliation…

However, he had absolutely *no* intention of going back down that road. His daughter, Emily, might be badly in need of a stable home environment, but there was absolutely no way he could ever face remarrying her neurotic, shallow and empty-headed mother.

He'd had several glamorous girlfriends since his wife had walked out all those years ago. But either he'd grown quickly tired of their company or they, too, had become fed up with always coming a bad second to his working life. In fact, Ace had never seen any reason to get married again—basically on the principle of 'once bitten…twice shy'. Not until his heart had been totally captured following that brief, quite extraordinary meeting with the bewitchingly lovely Eloise.

It was three long months since their passionate encounter, but he could still recall his delight at the miraculous way their two figures had seemed to fit so perfectly together, and the excitement of gently caressing her quivering, trembling flesh, which had almost seemed to melt beneath his fingers. If he closed his eyes, he could still smell the intoxicating, sweetly perfumed scent of her body, still hear her soft moans and breathless gasps of pleasure as their lovemaking had become more intense, both inciting and increasing his own fast-mounting desire.

Although he had tried to keep himself well under control, the thrillingly erotic, sensual touch of her hands and mouth on his body had overcome all restraint. Helplessly gripped by the fierce power of a deep primeval force, the like of which he'd never known before, he'd finally possessed her with a raging, thrusting urgency, the loud, pounding thud of her heart beating in rapid unison with his own as they'd both climaxed together in wave upon wave of ecstasy, before spiralling dizzily back down to earth.

Afterwards, as they'd lain entwined together in languorous warmth and tenderness, with Ace gently brushing tendrils of that wonderful fiery red hair from her damp brow, he'd known with absolute certainty that he had never, until that moment, experienced such overwhelming joy and happiness.

Try as he might, he'd been quite unable to forget the impact of that utterly astounding, spellbinding experience. Unfortunately, however much he might have loathed the idea, Ace had known that he had no choice but to return to his new, heavy responsibilities in England. It was also clear that, with the width of the

Atlantic Ocean as a permanent barrier between himself and Eloise, there could be no 'happy ever after' ending to their brief night of passion.

Besides, he was old enough to know that the sooner he did his best to put Eloise out of his mind, the better. There was obviously no way that they would ever meet again. And to be continually recalling the wondrous, soft quality of her skin, the truly dazzling heights which they'd attained in their lovemaking, could only make his present-day life even harder than it was already.

Lois gazed out of the window of the limousine as it sped along the motorway. The countryside was so different from that in the United States; it was taking her some time to get used to the very small scale of local geography here in England.

London, of course, had been great. When she'd first arrived in the country, some three weeks ago, she'd managed to find the time—amidst costume fittings, voice-coaching sessions and learning her script—to see the usual tourist sights of Buckingham Palace, the Tower and Westminster Abbey. But, this last week, which had been spent filming location shots outside various old houses all over the country, had been something else! In fact…

'You're going to *love* this house. It's far grander than the others we've used so far.'

'Hmm…?' Lois turned to look at her personal assistant, Peggy Fraser, who was leafing through a large file on her lap.

'Now…this is what I call a *real* stately home,' the English girl said, handing Lois a large black and white photograph.

'It certainly looks impressive,' Lois agreed, gazing at the picture of a classical Georgian-style Palladian mansion, whose entrance was dominated by huge stone pillars above a broad, sweeping expanse of wide stone steps. 'What's the interior like?'

'Absolutely frightful!' the other girl laughed. 'In fact, the main rooms are in a terrible state. But, as the producer says, that's all to the good. It's meant that we've had a completely free hand in the decoration.'

'Are we really staying there?' Lois frowned. 'It looks pretty uncomfortable to me. What's wrong with a nice, quiet local hotel?'

Peggy shrugged. 'I understand the film company negotiated a really good package deal with the owner. Which means that we can use practically the whole house—including all twenty-five bedrooms!—and the catering company will have masses of room in the enormous kitchens. In fact,' the small blonde girl added with a grin, 'I reckon it's going to be a lot of fun.'

'In your dreams!' Lois told her assistant gloomily. 'I'll lay you any odds that the plumbing will be practically non-existent. And I don't suppose that anyone will be too familiar with those important words ''constant hot water'', either!'

'Well, you may have a point,' Peggy admitted. 'But with the schedules having to be altered at the last minute…' She shrugged. 'I suppose this is the best that the production team could come up with under the circumstances.'

'I guess you're right,' Lois sighed, well aware that it was solely *her* fault that there had been such frantically hurried necessary changes in the film's shooting schedule.

Unfortunately, her appointment to see an eminent doctor in Harley Street, two weeks ago, had been fairly traumatic. Not being entirely a fool, she'd had a very good idea that he would confirm her suspicions. But, all the same…the whole scenario was definitely an earth-shattering one.

However, she was going to have to pull herself together pretty damn fast. Especially since the American backers of this new film had made it abundantly clear that the whole show was now riding on her slim shoulders.

'We know that you'll do us proud,' Sol Weiser had said, when she'd signed the contract some months ago, his wide, beaming smile not reflected in those cold, small piggy eyes. 'But, let's face it, darling—without your name on the credits, we wouldn't have dreamed of putting up the money for this arty type of film. So, we're all going to make sure it's a success, right?'

'I'll certainly do my best. It won't be my fault if this film bombs at the box office,' she'd told him with a confident smile.

However, after leaving his office, Lois had known that she wouldn't be human if she hadn't been plagued by doubts. Which had made it all the more nerve-racking when she'd had to phone Sol last week and tell him the news: she'd just discovered she was expecting a baby.

There had been an ominous silence for three days, before she'd heard that the film had been given the go-ahead. Although, in view of her changed circumstances, the schedule had been drastically altered.

'I'd like to pull the plug on this production,' Sol had told her, his voice heavy with disapproval. 'But the other backers seem to feel that if Madonna could manage to cope with the problem—and have such a great success with *Evita*—we ought to take a chance that you, too, can pull it off. But, I don't want any press exposure. So I expect everyone to keep their mouths buttoned up real tight. Do I make myself clear?' he'd added menacingly.

'As daylight,' she'd assured him fervently. 'After all,

Sol, I'm hardly likely to want to....' Her voice had faltered as she heard him slam down the phone.

So, now only the director, the producer and Peggy Fraser had been told the truth.

Peggy's involvement had been crucial, of course. Originally employed as the English costume designer, she'd also agreed to act as Lois' personal assistant, so as to keep the pregnancy as secret at possible.

As Peggy had pointed out, the fact that the film was set in the nineteenth century Regency period was going to be an enormous help. 'The high-waisted dresses of the time are just about perfect for your condition,' she'd told Lois during the costume fittings in London. 'We shouldn't have a problem disguising any thickening of your figure.'

Let's hope she's right, Lois told herself now, turning her head to gaze out of the window once more. Because she really wanted this film to be a great success.

Adapted from a short story by Jane Austen, written when the author was a young girl, *Lady Susan* should—if everything went according to plan—provide her with a golden opportunity to prove that she could extend her repertoire and succeed in playing a classic role. Lois had been excited by the screenplay—and the opportunity to play the lead part of Lady Susan: a heroine who was both diabolically attractive and, at the same time, a thoroughly wicked woman.

Quite apart from anything else, it certainly made a change from her more usual roles, playing feisty, go-getting modern heroines, along the lines of her last Oscar-winning movie.

Unfortunately, the Harley Street doctor's confirmation of what she'd suspected for the past few weeks had certainly thrown a spanner in the works.

Glancing down, Lois placed a hand on her stomach.

While her breasts had definitely increased in size, there didn't yet seem to be any other sign that she was now three months pregnant. And with a tight filming schedule she might still be able to get to the end of the shoot without anyone suspecting the truth. Besides, Sol's fellow backers had been right. If Madonna had managed to make the film of *Evita* while expecting a baby—then surely she, too, should be able to cope.

It was all the fault of that bout of illness which she'd suffered in India, Lois told herself grimly as the limousine left the motorway and began moving smoothly through the Sussex countryside.

Despite the fact that she'd never been in any way promiscuous, Lois had always believed in taking sensible, safe precautions against an unwanted or unplanned pregnancy. Unfortunately, as the doctor in London had so accurately pointed out, while the mini-pill would normally have provided adequate protection against any unforeseen accidents, her tummy upset in India had left her unwittingly vulnerable.

Which was why it had never occurred to her—not in a million years!—that the quite extraordinary and totally mind-blowing brief episode with the highly attractive Englishman could have resulted in her conceiving a child.

However, while the idea of having a baby had, quite frankly, come as a terrible shock, there was no way she could ever contemplate having an abortion. Nor did it seem right to even try and trace the father. Although there couldn't be too many Algernon Cedric Emersons hanging around England, she told herself wryly.

Besides, she could hardly blame Ace for the fact that they'd both been swept off their normally sane, sensible feet by an overwhelming tide of lust and desire. Since she had assured him that she was, as far as she knew at the time, taking adequate birth control precautions, it seemed totally wrong to expect Ace to carry any responsibility for the mess in which she now found herself.

What had happened was nothing more or less than a pure accident. And Lois had no doubts that she must be solely responsible for both the birth and upbringing of her child.

Leaning back in her seat, and resting her head against the soft leather upholstery, she gazed blindly past the dark figure of the chauffeur in the front of the vehicle. Oblivious of the green fields and small villages, her mind filled with memories of that extraordinary night of passion.

Goodness knows what it had been about Ace which had prompted her to so swiftly discard the cautious habits of a lifetime. Indeed, what had prompted her to behave and act so completely out of character was still a complete and utter mystery.

Maybe it was a legacy from her strict, God-fearing ancestors, who'd come to America from Europe at the beginning of the last century? Or perhaps it was her firm, no-nonsense upbringing by stern but loving parents? But, whatever the cause, she'd never felt at ease amongst those otherwise good friends who saw nothing wrong in hopping in and out of bed with complete strangers. She had always believed that a loving, long-term relationship was one thing—while a one-night stand was *quite* another.

And yet…how are the mighty fallen! Lois told herself with disgust. It certainly looked as though little Snow White had now 'drifted' more than somewhat!

Goodness knows why she'd behaved so totally out of character. Maybe it was something to do with the dangerous gleam in his sleepy-looking hooded grey eyes? But it had merely taken one glance at the tall, dynamically attractive Englishman—and she'd immediately taken leave of her senses!

Even when he'd been carrying her back to her small cottage on the beach, Lois had felt a desperate urge to remain clasped in his arms, and had felt almost totally bereft when he'd left her alone in the bedroom to call for the doctor.

Of course, the brandy she'd tossed so happily down her throat hadn't helped the situation. She was normally only used to drinking a glass or two of wine, and the strong alcohol had seemed to release all her inhibitions. When he'd gathered her into his embrace, possessing her lips in such a tender, heart-stopping kiss, she'd…well, there was simply no other way of putting it…she'd totally lost *all* control.

Quickly shutting her eyes, it was all Lois could do not to moan out loud, as she recalled the exquisite warmth of his mouth on hers, the ever-increasing passion and desire, flashing like forked lightning through her entire being as she responded helplessly to the seductive, feather-light touch of his fingers tracing patterns of fire on her quivering flesh.

Firmly in the grip of a shuddering excitement at the feel of his naked, hard-muscled figure pressed closely to her own trembling body, she'd feverishly responded to his softly whispered murmurs of delight as his mouth and hands had moved so erotically over her quivering flesh. Nor, however much she had tried, could she forget the moment of his possession, the vortex of spiralling excitement produced by the hard, pulsating rhythm, until her world had seemed to explode in an amazing fireburst of convulsive, shuddering pleasure so intense that it had been almost more than she could bear.

Later, as she had lain sleepily enfolded in his arms, his fingers gently brushing the damp curls from her brow, she couldn't recall ever feeling such happiness and contentment. But, waking with the dawn to find him gone, she had known—even as she'd wept painful, bitter tears—that he had done them both a favour.

Since they clearly came from two very different worlds, it would never be possible to recapture the joy they had experienced together. And even when Lois had discovered she was expecting his baby she had instinctively known that she must never hark back, regretting what might have been, but look forward to cherishing the new life which lay within her.

'It seems as though we're arrived at last.' Peggy's voice broke into her thoughts, and Lois looked up to see that their vehicle was now slowing down. Turning off the main road, the limousine drove past two small houses, standing guard on either side of a pair of large wrought-iron gates. It moved slowly down a long gravelled drive, and she noticed that they were surrounded by a large park dotted with clumps of tall oak trees.

'It certainly looks like my idea of a grand English country estate,' Lois said, smiling at the sight of a flock of sheep busy nibbling the long, lush green grass.

'But all the same,' she continued, her gaze narrowing as she peered through the open window, 'I can't help feeling it all looks just a bit...well, a bit run-down, if you know what I mean?'

'You're right,' the other girl agreed, staring out at the sight of long, uncut grass swaying in the slight afternoon breeze. 'However, the producer, Dave Green, was telling me that they'd chosen this location just *because* it looked so authentic. And, when you think about it, I suppose it's obvious, really.'

When Lois turned to look at her in surprise, Peggy explained, 'It didn't occur to me, either. But of course there were no mowing machines in the eighteenth century. In fact, if anyone had wanted to cut the grass, it would have needed a large gang of men with scythes to do the job. Incidentally, I hear that the director is intending to add that sort of background, rural type of scene to the film schedule. Maybe shooting it some time next week.'

'It's amazing that just one family should live in such a large house,' Lois murmured as the limousine swept up to the front of the house, dominated by the large stone pillars.

'Well, they obviously aren't living too well at the moment,' the other girl pointed out as she gathered her papers and files together. 'So, maybe the owner has fallen on hard times? Because Dave told me that Lord Ratcliffe is quite happy for us to do anything we like with the house and grounds,' she added as the chauffeur came around to open the door and help them with their bags. 'Which is fair enough, considering it's costing the film company a staggering amount of money to hire this place.'

'It certainly looks as if he's going to need every dime he can lay his hands on,' Lois agreed dryly as she gazed at the crumbling stonework and badly cracked flight of steps leading up to the front door.

Preceded by the chauffeur, carrying their suitcases into the house, Lois found herself amongst a crowd of actors, half of whom were in costume, all milling around the vast hall.

'Lovely to see you, darling,' the producer called out, hurrying through the noisy throng to greet her. 'You're looking *great*!' he added, clearly relieved to note that the beautiful girl, casually dressed in slim-cut jeans and a white T-shirt under a navy blue blazer, didn't seem to have put on an ounce of weight.

'How's everything going?' she asked, staring up at the heavily decorated plaster ceiling.

'Amazingly, we appear to be on schedule at the moment. Our beloved director, Peter, is busy rehearsing a scene in the Orangery at the moment. But he's looking forward to seeing you at dinner tonight,' he said, taking hold of her arm and warning her to be careful of the thick, electrical cables littering the marble floor. 'Far more to the point, darling…how are *you* feeling?' He grinned. 'No morning sickness, I hope?'

'For heaven's sake—keep your voice down!' she warned him grimly. 'I hope you realise that if word gets out, Sol will be only too happy to pull the plug on this film. So, let's cut out the wisecracks—huh?'

'Oops! I'm sorry. You're absolutely right,' Dave admitted, the smile quickly wiped from his face at the thought of invoking Sol Weiser's wrath. 'Ah, there's our host, Lord Ratcliffe,' he added, obviously glad to change the subject as he waved at a tall figure standing in a doorway on the other side of the vast hall.

'What's he like?'

'Absolutely *divine*! All the girls have fallen *madly* in love with our noble lord—and I bet you will, too!'

'Ha-ha!' she retorted, feeling too tired after the journey to put up with any of Dave's usual camp style. Especially since she happened to know that he was a happily married man, and crazy about his two young children.

'No, really, I'm not joking. Well…not entirely,' Dave said as he led her across the room. 'For instance, I'm sorry to have to tell you that Lord Ratcliffe is *far* more impressive than your leading man in this film.'

'Oh, come on—there's nothing wrong with Neil Gray,' she protested. 'In fact, he's a damn good actor.'

Dave shrugged. 'I'm not knocking Neil. It's just that this guy has definitely got a lot more going for him.'

'Oh, yeah...?' Lois snorted derisively. But she didn't have an opportunity to say any more as she was suddenly swept up in a large bear-hug from a well-known character actor whom she hadn't seen for some years.

Busy catching up on his news, she was slightly irritated to find her arm being tugged by Dave.

'Come on, Lois,' he called out over the general hubbub, dragging her over to the tall, dark-haired man standing beside a marble column. 'I'd like to introduce you to—'

'For heaven's sake, Dave, you might have let me finish talking to Bart. It's years since we've seen one another.'

'Lord Ratcliffe,' the producer continued, taking no notice of her protest as he turned to their host. 'I don't think you've yet had the pleasure of meeting our famous leading lady—Miss Lois Shelton.'

It was clearly a close call as to which of the two people concerned looked the most stunned.

For her part, Lois knew that she ought to have the advantage in this sort of situation. Surely all those years of acting so many parts should have enabled her to swiftly assume an expression of polite disinterest?

Unfortunately, she couldn't seem to get a firm grip on herself. Perhaps she was hallucinating? Because, although it couldn't possibly be true...it definitely looked as if... *Oh my God*! What in the hell do I do now? she asked herself desperately, suddenly feeling sick as she realised that it really *was* Ace who was now staring down at her; the blood draining swiftly from his face, as if he'd just seen a ghost.

With harsh, cold reality beginning to break through

the chaos and turmoil in her mind, Lois made a determined effort to pull herself together.

However weird or totally bizarre such a coincidence might be, she was going to have to face the fact that this man—with whom she'd had a brief, passionate encounter in the Philippines—was not just some anonymous English lawyer. Unfortunately, it now seemed that he was, in reality, Lord Ratcliffe, the owner of this huge old house.

It felt as if she had been standing here, in a state of numb disbelief, for an enormous length of time. However, she realised that she could only have been mentally paralysed for just a few seconds. With Dave continuing to chatter away, nineteen to the dozen, Lois gradually began to get a grip on her muzzy brain. While the man she'd known as Ace, remained staring down at her; his hawk-like features frozen into an expression of utter shock and bewilderment.

And it was the sight of Lord Ratcliffe—as she was now clearly going to have to call him—which helped her to make the first move.

Instinctively taking pity on the poor man—who looked as if he might expire from a heart attack any minute—Lois took a step forward and put out her hand.

'How do you do, Lord Ratcliffe?' she murmured, carefully avoiding his eyes. 'It's…um…it's very nice to meet you.'

Clearly making a supreme effort to gather his scattered wits, Ace at last managed to find his voice.

'I don't think "very nice" are exactly the words *I* would use, Miss…er…Miss Shelton,' he drawled slowly, gallantly raising her hand to his lips.

'In fact, as far as I'm concerned,' he added, the heavy-lidded, clear grey eyes now glinting with wry, sardonic amusement, 'that well-known phrase "enchanted to meet you" would seem to be *far* more appropriate!'

CHAPTER THREE

'I DON'T know about you—but I'm completely lost!'

'You're not the only one,' Lois muttered as she and Peggy, accompanied by two sturdy men carrying their luggage, followed the producer's assistant up yet another long flight of stairs.

Downstairs, in the large hall, she'd been so anxious to escape from the shockingly unexpected, completely unnerving encounter with Ace that she couldn't have cared less *where* she was being taken. But this long hike through dusty back passages, up stairs and along corridors—mostly lined with gloomy ancestral portraits—was definitely beginning to get her down.

'Here we are,' the assistant announced, consulting a list on the clipboard in her hands as they at last came to a halt by a grand, impressively large pair of double doors.

'I'm sorry we had to make such a long detour, because of all the electrical cables and camera equipment,' the girl continued, moving aside to allow one of the men to carry Lois' suitcases through into the room, 'however, Dave Green wanted you to have the very best accommodation. And this, so I'm told, is the Grand State Bedroom, originally designed in the eighteenth century for visiting royalty.'

'*Crumbs…!*' Peggy gasped as she and Lois followed the girl into the large room. 'Did any kings and queens *really* sleep in here?'

'No, I believe it was more a case of having a special room available—just in case they might want to spend a night at Ratcliffe Hall,' the assistant said, before once again consulting her clipboard. 'And now, Miss Fraser, I'll show you to your bedroom. We're running a little behind time, so…'

'Well, I…er…I'll see you later,' Peggy muttered, casting a nervous glance at Lois—who'd remained utterly silent since they'd entered the room—before hurrying after the assistant, who was now moving swiftly on down the corridor.

Left on her own, Lois quickly closed her eyes and counted up to ten. Unfortunately, when she opened them again, her fervent hope that she'd been hallucinating was quickly dispelled. It was not a psychedelic dream. She really *was* standing in the midst of what could only be described as a total nightmare.

Gazing in horrified astonishment around the enormous room, her eyes were immediately drawn to the truly massive four-poster bed, set up on a high dias. Heavily festooned with thick satin swags, tails and drapes, in a depressing shade of deep crimson edged with wide, dark gold fringing, the whole monstrous edifice was topped by tall sprays of red and gold ostrich feather plumes at each of the four corners.

'Oh, *Lord*!' she muttered helplessly, turning her head to stare with dismay at the walls, covered with the same dark red satin, on which were hung many large, sombre portraits of grim-faced men and women, all dressed in costumes of a bygone age. And the bare, dark oak boards covering the floor did little to make the huge, formal room look more comfortable, either. Even the heavy, crimson satin curtains—draped in such a way over the windows as to exclude most of the warm afternoon sun—contributed to the general atmosphere of doom and gloom.

Her heart sinking down into her boots, Lois told herself that she'd *never* seen such a deeply depressing room. In fact, all this place needed were several large cobwebs hanging from that awful bed and it would be a perfect setting for a horror movie!

The adjacent bathroom was no better. All her bad vibes and dark suspicions about the lack of modern plumbing were amply confirmed as she peered gingerly around the door, her eyes widening at the sight of the ancient bathtub—into which, she was convinced, three or four grown men could have fitted with ease.

Moving closer, she stared in bewilderment at a complicated-looking semi-circular steel structure, enclosing one end of the bath. At least six or seven feet high, it appeared to have many old-fashioned white china handles and knobs, labelled with words such as 'spray', 'jet' and 'douche'. But it wasn't until Lois noticed a large object at the top of the massive edifice—a twelve-inch-diameter circle of metal, covered in holes—that light slowly began to dawn.

'Good heavens…it must be some kind of shower!' she breathed, taking a step back to view the complicated, dangerous-looking contraption with a mixture of incredulity and horror.

Trailing slowly back into the gloomy bedroom, Lois gave a heavy sigh. The thought of having to spend even *one* night in this ghastly room—not to mention that bathroom, clearly dating from the dawn of time—was bad enough. But to have to put up with it for six weeks…? *No way*!

On the other hand, she really didn't need the likely hassle involved in trying to change her room.

In the movie business there were many actresses who'd managed to get themselves a bad reputation by acting like thoroughly spoilt children. And, since most people seemed only too willing to believe the worst, she'd always done her best to avoid being known as a prima donna. Unfortunately, and however unfair it might be, she knew that if she did complain about this bedroom the word would soon get around that Lois Shelton was nothing but a pain in the butt.

Either way—you just can't win! she told herself with another heavy sigh.

But, hey! This awful bedroom was the very least of her problems, right? She had far more important things to worry about, Lois reminded herself grimly, pacing restlessly up and down the room. Such as, what in the heck she was going to do about her utterly unexpected reunion with Ace...?

Try as she might, Lois couldn't seem to get a firm grip on the situation. Talk about the fickle finger of fate! How was it possible that a man whom she'd only met once—on the other side of the world, for heaven's sake!—should now turn out to be some kind of aristocrat, and the owner of this huge old house?

Standing downstairs in the hall, amidst all the noise of actors and film crew eddying about their still figures, Lois had found herself desperately praying for divine intervention. Goodness knows, she wasn't choosy; a thunderbolt striking Ace's tall figure, or the marble flooring giving way beneath her own trembling feet would have done equally well.

But clearly her guardian angel had been asleep on the job. Because Ace, seemingly recovering at the speed of light from their shocking confrontation, had proceeded to give her a really, *really* hard time.

'I'm delighted to be able to welcome such a famous film star to my humble abode,' he'd drawled coolly, his grey eyes beneath their heavy lids gleaming with unconcealed mockery.

Who's he kidding? There's nothing 'humble' about

this particular abode! she'd told herself grimly, instinctively trying to remove her hand from his warm clasp.

'And what an interesting name you have. I don't think I've ever had the pleasure of meeting anyone called Lois,' he'd continued smoothly.

'Oh, really...?' she'd muttered warily, feeling sick to the pit of her stomach with nerves, and...and the same kind of strange, sexual excitement which she'd felt when first setting eyes on him three months ago.

'Maybe it's an American version of the French *Eloise...*?' the foul man had continued inexorably, his lips twitching in silent humour at the brief expression of horrified panic which had flashed across her pale cheeks. 'Now *that's* a very pretty name. What do you think?'

Lois had responded with a nervous trill of laughter, which even to her ears had sounded far too high-pitched and shrill.

'Well, I'm afraid that I...I really don't have any views on the subject,' she'd murmured nervously, before turning in desperation to smile at the producer, Dave Green.

'I'm...er...I'm feeling a bit tired after the journey, Dave,' she'd said, still trying to surreptitiously tug her fingers away from Ace's firm grip. 'I'd like to freshen up a bit before meeting the rest of the cast. So, is it possible to see my room, and...?'

'Oh, sure.' Dave had beckoned across the room to one of his female assistants. 'Joan is in charge of all the household arrangements. She'll show you to your bedroom. And if you need anything, don't hesitate to let her know, OK?'

'Well, its been really interesting to meet you, Lord Ratcliffe,' Lois had said, almost sagging with relief as they were joined by the producer's assistant. 'We're all going to be very busy for the next six weeks. So, I don't suppose we'll have the opportunity to see much of each

other,' she'd added firmly, hoping that Ace would get
the message.

Unfortunately, the awful man clearly wasn't prepared
to take a blind bit of notice of any 'message'.

'No, I think you're mistaken,' he'd drawled smoothly,
and her cheeks had flushed at the clear note of sardonic
amusement in his voice as he'd drawn her closer to his
tall figure. 'In fact, I'm quite sure there will be many
opportunities to renew our…er…brief acquaintance,'
he'd added, a distinct note of silky menace in his voice
as he'd once more raised her hand to his warm lips,
before at last setting her free.

I definitely know a threat when I hear one! Lois told
herself grimly, as she now paced up and down the dreadful red room. What was more—although she could have
been mistaken—she was sure that she'd heard Ace add,
under his breath, *'And that's a promise!'* as he'd let go
of her hand.

It was all so damn unfair! One moment she'd been
confidently looking forward to joining her colleagues on
an interesting film, and then—in the twinkling of an
eye—she'd suddenly found herself well and truly up the
creek without a paddle! What had *she* ever done to deserve such rotten bad luck? And why, now she came to
think about it, had Ace been lying through his teeth…?

Like all actresses, who had to memorise a vast number
of play and film scripts, she had a very good memory.
Which meant that she was darned certain that in the
Philippines Ace had referred to himself as a 'boring lawyer'. So why pretend to be something he wasn't? Did
he imagine that she would have been be all over him
like a rash if she'd known he was a member of the
British aristocracy? Because, if so, he was badly mistaken. She didn't give two hoots about that sort of thing.

Unfortunately, as a small voice in her head kept pointing out, it probably wouldn't have made any difference if Ace had announced that he was the Archangel Gabriel! Because the hard, unpalatable truth was that from the first moment she'd set eyes on the guy she'd *completely* lost her marbles!

Her face flaming with embarrassment and mortification, Lois was still trying to think what she was going to do about the dreadful situation in which she now found herself when there was a loud knock.

'Hello…' A young girl peered around the door. 'I've been asked to place these in here,' she said, entering the room with a large vase of pink roses in her hands.

'How kind. Thank you…er…'

'My name's Emily,' the girl told her with a shy smile. 'I'm the "gofer" on this film.'

Lois smiled at the note of pride and excitement in the girl's voice. 'As in "gofer" this…and "gofer" that…?'

'You're absolutely right.' Emily grinned. 'It's a really cool job. All my friends at school are dead jealous. I can't wait to tell them that I've met you. They'll go absolutely bananas!'

It was the mention of school which prompted Lois to look closer at the girl, whom she now realised couldn't be more than fourteen.

Tall and gawky, with stick-thin arms and legs, it had to be said that Emily looked a bit of a mess. Dark spiky hair—clearly cut with a very blunt pair of scissors—and a ring through the side of her nose did nothing to enhance the girl's appearance. While the tight black T-shirt clinging to her skinny frame over a very short black skirt and black tights ending in heavy Doc Marten boots, were clearly designed to make the statement: 'Rebellious Teenager'.

Only the girl's sweet smile in her heart-shaped face,

and a pair of large grey eyes heavily fringed with dark eyelashes, gave some promise of future beauty.

'Where would you like me to put the flowers?'

Lois shrugged as she looked helplessly around the room. 'How about over there…?' She nodded towards a large mahogany chest of drawers, heavily encrusted with ormolu mounts.

'OK,' Emily agreed cheerfully, her heavy boots clumping over the floorboards as she carefully carried the vase across the room. 'Oh, wow! This place is really…well, it's really something else, isn't it?' she added, gazing around in frank amazement.

'You're so right!' Lois agreed glumly, her lips relaxing into a grin as Emily stared with wide-eyed fascination at the huge ostrich feather plumes on top of the four-poster.

'I only arrived a few days ago, so I haven't been in here before now,' Emily said, going over to clamber up onto the bed. 'Some of the other bedrooms are absolutely the pits. There's one done out in gloomy dark green velvet which is *really* scary!' she added, bouncing up and down on the mattress. 'But I expect you've been given the State Bedroom because you're such a famous film star, and all.'

'Famous or not—I'd be far happier with a much smaller room…*and* some decent plumbing,' Lois sighed.

'You're not the only one!' Emily grinned. 'Dad keeps going berserk about not having enough hot water. And the production crew aren't too happy, either. Although it's not so bad in our wing of the house. I'm sure Dad won't mind if you want to use my bathroom.'

'That's a kind offer. I'll definitely think about it,' Lois murmured, wondering how on earth this very chatty, weird-looking young schoolgirl had managed to find a job with the film unit.

And who on earth was 'Dad'? Lois wondered as the girl continued to use the awful bed as some kind of trampoline. It would obviously have to be a senior executive. So, maybe Peter Danvers, the director of this film, was the most likely candidate...?

'Wow! This is really brilliant,' Emily laughed as she bounced higher and higher. 'Absolutely wicked!'

'Be careful!' Lois warned as the massive structure creaked and groaned beneath the assault. 'By the way,' she added with a slight frown as Emily ceased her bouncing, 'it's still only June. Shouldn't you still be at school...?'

'You're right.' The girl grinned. 'But luckily I managed to get myself suspended for a few weeks.'

'Suspended, huh?' Lois muttered, looking in her purse for the keys to her luggage. 'Is that regarded as a bad thing here in England?'

'Well, it's not exactly *good* news,' Emily admitted with a careless shrug. 'All the same, I think it's really *pathetic* of the school to take that sort of action—just because I lost my temper and swore at one of the teachers.'

'Well...' Lois hesitated, trying to recall her own attitude to school life at the age of fourteen. 'I agree that it doesn't sound like a really bad crime. But, if you'll forgive me for saying so, I can't help feeling sorry for your teacher. After all,' she added with a shrug, 'it must be a real drag having to teach kids your age. Especially when all you're likely to care about are clothes, pop music and boyfriends. So, I expect your teacher found being sworn at just about the last straw.'

There was a long silence as Emily considered the matter. 'I hadn't thought about that,' she said slowly. 'I suppose you're right. Anyway, Dad tore me off a terrific strip about it, and my mother wasn't too pleased, either.'

'Never mind. I don't suppose you'll make the same mistake again.' Lois grinned over at the girl, who was looking slightly crestfallen. 'Besides, as you so rightly said, it has resulted in you getting a job on this film. Are you enjoying yourself?'

'Oh, yes—it's really great!' Emily gave her a happy grin. 'And *much* more interesting and glamorous than the pop music scene. I want to be a film star when I grow up,' she confided.

'It's mostly hard work—and very little glamour, I'm afraid,' Lois muttered, still wondering where she had put her keys as she searched through the pockets of her jacket.

'Mummy says that I haven't a chance, because you have to be very good-looking. Of course,' the girl added reflectively, 'Mummy *is* very beautiful. She used to be a model, and had her picture on the front of lots of expensive magazines.'

'Good for her,' Lois murmured, wondering how to get rid of Emily without hurting the youngster's feelings. 'However, looks aren't everything. You also need a considerable amount of talent. And now, if you don't mind…'

'Hi, Dad!' Emily suddenly called out, jumping off the bed and bounding across the room like a puppy towards the tall figure of a man standing in the open doorway.

'I did knock. But Emily was making such a noise, you obviously didn't hear me,' Ace said with a slight smile as the young girl threw her arms around his waist. 'I merely called by just to see if you were comfortable, and…' His voice died away as he gazed around the room, his expression mirroring that of Lois when she, too, had first entered the depressing red bedroom.

'*Good God*! I'd forgotten about this *ghastly* room!' he exclaimed, staring in appalled fascination at the massive four-poster bed. 'Surely nobody expects you to sleep in that monstrosity?'

But Lois wasn't listening. Her body and mind had frozen as she stood rooted to the spot, staring blankly across the room.

Why…*why* had it never occurred to her that Ace was likely to be a married man? And if she'd had any sense—or had given the matter even a moment's thought—surely she ought to have realised that he was also likely to have children?

Because there was absolutely no doubt that she was now looking at father and daughter. Emily not only had the same shade of dark hair, but she'd also inherited her father's grey eyes and his tall, rangy frame.

Feeling sick, both at her own stupidity and at the fact that the current scenario seemed to be getting even more complicated every minute, Lois struggled to pull herself together.

Keep calm! You've got to keep very, *very* cool, calm and collected, she told herself desperately. There was absolutely nothing she could do, or say, in such a fraught situation. Well, not at the moment, anyway. Later, when some form of life came back to her frozen limbs, she would hopefully be able to find a way of coping with this fresh disaster. But in the meantime, if she kept very quiet…and very still…maybe it would all prove to be nothing but a terrible nightmare?

'I'm sorry. As I'm sure you've discovered—a little of Emily goes a long way!' Ace drawled, his dark brows drawing together in a frown as he viewed the pale, strained expression on the face of the girl standing across the room.

How anyone had the nerve to put this beautiful creature in these awful surroundings he had no idea. But he was obviously going to have to sort out this stupid mistake as quickly as possible.

'I imagine you must be tired after your journey,' he continued, firmly taking hold of Emily by the arm. 'We'll look forward to seeing you at dinner.'

Remaining silent, and still rooted to the spot, Lois could only give a weak nod of her head before father and daughter left the room, closing the door quietly behind them.

Maybe it was the sort of thing that happened in pregnancy, but she couldn't *ever* remember feeling quite so tired and weary as she did at this moment. So much seemed to have happened, in such a short space of time, that she just couldn't seem to cope with this new problem. Not on top of everything else. And, while the thought of having to spend a night in that awful bed was enough to give her the heebie-jeebies, Lois knew that if she didn't make an effort to relax—and have a quick nap—she was going to collapse from sheer mental and physical exhaustion.

A few moments later, as she lay curled up on the hideous, deep crimson bed cover, beneath the soft mohair comfort of her own lightweight travelling rug, she breathed a deep sigh of relief. At least she was now horizontal and, with any luck, would soon be totally unconscious.

But, as she slowly drifted off to sleep, Emily's references to 'Mummy' kept drifting through her weary mind. Which could only mean, on top of everything else, that she was also going to have to cope with meeting Ace's wife.

First Ross Whitney—and now Ace Ratcliffe. Why...oh, *why* did she keep falling for married men? was her last, despairing thought before falling into a deep sleep.

Slowly dragging a brush through the tangled curls of her fiery red hair, Lois flinched as she stared at herself in the mirror.

Where on earth, she wondered, was the woman who'd arrived earlier today at Ratcliffe Hall? Was it possible that this exhausted, pale-faced creature gazing so wearily back at her was one and the same person?

Only this morning she'd felt full of confidence, and looking forward to the next six weeks working with so many of her old friends and colleagues. But now, gazing at the apprehensive, nervous expression in the troubled blue eyes, she totally failed to recognise her former self.

Was this trip to England turning into a truly awful, disastrous can of worms—or what? In fact, the only cheerful note in an otherwise utterly dire scenario was the fact that she no longer faced the prospect of having to spend the next six weeks in that dreadful State Bedroom.

After falling quickly asleep, it had seemed only minutes later that she'd found herself being shaken awake by Peggy.

From what she had been able to make out, it appeared that following his brief visit to her room Ace had angrily demanded the attendance in his private study of both the film's producer and director.

'You must have made a really *terrific* impression on Lord Ratcliffe,' Peggy had giggled. 'Because I hear that he hit the roof on the subject of film executives who didn't know how to look after their leading ladies. Apparently both Dave and Peter Danvers emerged looking positively white and shaking!'

Lois had been feeling too tired and exhausted at the time to do or say anything—other than allow herself to be transported lock, stock and barrel to her new accommodation, in Lord Ratcliffe's own personal wing of the enormous mansion. However, there was no doubt that she *was* now going to be far more comfortable. Not to mention being able to get a good night's sleep.

Turning around, Lois gazed with considerable pleasure at her new surroundings. Above a plain white dado and chair rail, the walls were covered with a pale cream silk shantung, the same material being used to line the pale blue silk curtains which hung at each end of the bed. But what a contrast between *this* four-poster, and that other grim monstrosity! This bed, with its elegant, delicately carved pale wood posts, was topped by a lightly scalloped canopy edged with pale blue and cream fringing—the same pale blue used to cover the two comfortable armchairs on the thick, cream-coloured carpet.

However, while she might now have much to be thankful for—particularly the ultra-modern, *en suite* bathroom!—Lois knew that everything else in her life was still fraught with major problems.

It had, of course, been the most terrific shock to meet Ace again, and in such extraordinary circumstances. Unfortunately, it wasn't helping this potentially highly embarrassing situation to discover that she still found him diabolically attractive. And quite *why* he'd been so secretive about his ownership of this huge mansion, and his title, she had absolutely no idea.

On the other hand…Lois had to admit that she'd been equally cautious. Because, while she had indeed been christened Eloise, it wasn't the name by which she was now known. And, since neither of them had volunteered any information about their surnames, or marital status, maybe she was being just a little hard on Ace…?

However, any question about whether they should or shouldn't have had disclosed more of their individual backgrounds was now irrelevant. The only thing which *really* mattered was that she was now pregnant with

Ace's child. A fact which could, if she wasn't very careful, have dire consequences for both the future of this film and all the people working on it.

Sol Weiser—chiefly concerned about any possible scandal—had, of course, demanded to know the name of the baby's father. A demand which had placed Lois in a very difficult position. Which was why, needing to quickly set the American financier's mind at rest, she'd told him that her lover had absolutely *no* connection with show business, and that the affair was long over. Sol hadn't been at all happy about the situation. But he'd reluctantly accepted her assurances—which, at the time, had been the absolute truth.

Unfortunately, the situation was now dramatically changed. With Sol looking for an excuse to pull the rug out from beneath this film—which he hadn't wanted to finance in the first place—Lois knew that Ace must *never* discover that he was the father of her baby. Because, while she had no idea how he would react to the news, she couldn't afford to have any loose talk about her condition—either buzzing around the film set or appearing in the newspapers. Which meant that it was desperately important to keep her secret well under wraps.

However, with any luck she'd have finished filming and be on her way back to America before the news broke. After all, she comforted herself, it was only a matter of staggering through the next six weeks. If she was very careful to watch her diet and not put on any weight, there was no reason why anyone should guess the truth.

A loud knock interrupted her thoughts, and she turned to see Emily's head appearing around the side of the door. 'Dad said you might get lost. So he's asked me to show you the way downstairs,' the girl said, looking around the room. 'This bedroom is a lot better, isn't it?'

'It sure is!' Lois grinned, putting down her hairbrush and giving her make-up a last quick glance before rising to her feet. 'Please thank your father for arranging everything,' she added, anxious to have as little contact with Ace in the future as possible.

Unfortunately, her hopes were dashed as Emily informed her that she'd be able to thank him herself, since he was joining them for dinner. 'You look absolutely brilliant—really wicked!' the girl added, gazing with youthful admiration at the film star's aquamarine blue silk shirt over slim black leggings.

'I phoned my best friend and told her that you're dead glamorous,' Emily confided artlessly as she led the way out of the room. 'She nearly had a fit. Talk about being jealous! And Mummy is going bananas, too. She's practically foaming at the mouth with frustration—and can't wait to meet all the film crew.'

Oh, Lord! Lois thought, feeling quite sick at the prospect of having to meet this young girl's mother. If she'd known that Ace was a married man, she'd *never* have behaved so badly three months ago. In fact...

'I think this is the right way,' Emily muttered, pausing for a moment before turning left to lead Lois down the long corridor. 'I still manage to get lost, since I've only been here for a few days,' she explained. 'And Dad's not much better, either. He says that there are still lots of rooms he's hardly seen.'

Lois glanced at her with a puzzled frown. 'Surely your father must know this house like the back of his hand?'

Emily shook her head. 'No, old Great-Uncle Hector only died a few months ago. Apparently he and my dad never really got on. So, when Dad inherited this house, he hadn't a clue about the place. He's not too keen about the title, either.' She giggled. 'But I think it's quite cool. Especially as I'm now an "Honourable"!'

'A what...?'

Emily shrugged her thin shoulders as she led the way down a huge, sweeping staircase. 'Well, it's only a courtesy title—and just a bit of a laugh, really. But of course Mummy is absolutely *furious* about not being a real Lady! I don't get on too well with my mother,' she explained, bounding down the stairs ahead of Lois. 'But Dad says that's just a sort of adolescent, generation gap thing.'

'I'm sure he's quite right,' Lois muttered, trying to make some sort of sense out of the youngster's artless flow of words. 'I don't quite understand...? Are you saying that your father has only recently inherited this house?'

Emily nodded. 'He used to be a big hot-shot lawyer in London. But now he's stuck with this awful old place. He calls it a "damned huge mausoleum".' She giggled. 'But, even though he grumbles a lot about it, I think he's quite enjoying having to live deep in the countryside and learn all about farming.'

'And how do you feel about it?'

'Well, it's all right for Dad—he's old and past it.' The girl shrugged, casually consigning her father to the dump-bin of ancient history. 'But I reckon the countryside is the absolute pits! Do you know, there isn't a cinema—or even a decent video shop?—for miles and miles,' she added in horrified tones. 'London's where it's at. At least I've got some friends of my own age living there.'

'Haven't you any brothers or sisters?'

Emily shook her head. 'I wouldn't mind having a sister. But now, of course, what Dad really *needs* is a son.'

'Why should he need a son...?' Lois echoed blankly,

feeling as if she'd somehow wandered into a strange, Alice in Wonderland world, where everyone else seemed to speak a different language.

'To inherit the title, of course!' Emily sighed, rolling her eyes to heaven at the dimness of some grown-ups as she pushed open a large, green baize-covered door and ran ahead down a wide, stone-flagged passage to the large kitchen.

Would this meal never end? Lois asked herself glumly. Leaning back in her chair and allowing the sounds of conversation and raucous laughter to flow over her head, she tried to think what to do about her increasingly difficult situation.

Throughout the evening she'd been careful to avoid any eye contact with Ace, sitting at the far end of the massively long, scrubbed pine kitchen table. Nevertheless, Lois had been fully aware at all times of his dynamically masculine figure, and the many glances despatched in her direction by those grey eyes, glinting with wry amusement beneath their heavy lids.

He might find something humorous about this situation—but he doesn't know the half of it, she told herself grimly. Telling his wife and daughter that I'm now expecting his baby would soon wipe that sardonic smile off his arrogant face!

Not, that she'd *ever* do such a terrible thing, Lois quickly corrected herself, ashamed of even thinking such an unworthy thought. Besides, the most important thing on her mind at the moment was to make sure that Ace *didn't* discover the truth about her condition.

Stifling a weary yawn, she wondered again if it was her pregnancy which was causing her to feel so tired and exhausted a lot of the time. Because she usually had an enormous amount of energy—an absolutely essential ingredient for anyone in the film business. Getting up at four or five in the morning, to be on set ready for make-up, was no joke. It required a quiet, disciplined life and, most important of all, a strong, healthy body. Which was just what she didn't seem to have at the moment, she thought, suddenly assailed by a brief feeling of nausea.

Slowly sipping a glass of water, and determined not to give in to any weakness, Lois turned as the stout, sturdy figure of an elderly woman settled down in the vacant chair beside her.

'Are you all right, dearie?' the woman asked, her dark, twinkling little boot-button eyes gazing searchingly at the pale, strained features of the beautiful red-headed girl.

'Yes, yes…I'm fine,' Lois murmured, suddenly real-ising that she did indeed, feel a whole lot better. Maybe that slight wave of nausea had been caused by something she'd eaten—nothing to do with the baby? 'I don't think we've met,' she added, smiling at the plump, elderly figure beside her.

'Nor we have,' the woman agreed. 'Of course I know who *you* are, seeing as how my late husband, Fred, used to be one of your biggest fans,' she added with an in-fectious chuckle of laughter. 'However, the name's Nora, dearie. Mrs Nora Barker.'

'Well, it's nice to meet you, Nora. Are you anything to do with this film?'

The woman laughed. 'Good Lord, no! His nibs has just dragged me out of retirement, to help run this house,' she explained, nodding to where Ace sat at the other end of the table. 'I used to be his old nanny—and now I'm his new housekeeper. So, it looks as though we've both gone up the world, doesn't it?'

Lois couldn't help grinning as the elderly woman gave another burst of rollicking laughter. She didn't know anything about English domestic servants—but this woman was clearly an unusual character.

'I hear his nibs got you out of that nasty State Bedroom—and a good thing too. You'll be much more comfortable in *our* side of the house,' the housekeeper told Lois, giving the younger woman another keen, searching glance before rising slowly to her feet. 'If you need anything—anything at all—you just let me know. All right, dearie?'

Lois smiled. 'Yes, Nora, I'll definitely give you a shout if I need anything,' she said, deciding that she really liked this plump, comfortable-looking woman, who clearly had her feet very firmly planted on the ground.

Which was more than could be said for the majority of the people in the film world, she thought, glancing idly around the tables in the huge medieval-looking kitchen. However, the crew on this film seemed to be a sensible bunch. With everyone aware of an early call in the morning, there was very little evidence of any hard drinking. And if she, too, was due to be on set first thing tomorrow, maybe it would be a good idea to slip away as soon as possible…?

Glancing through her eyelashes at the tall figure of Ace, as he bent his dark, arrogant head towards one of the young, pretty actresses sitting beside him, Lois decided that this was clearly as good a time as any.

Having made what she hoped was an inconspicuous exit from the kitchen, she walked swiftly down the stone-paved corridor to the hall. However, while looking for the light switch—and congratulating herself on having successfully avoided Ace—she nearly jumped out of her skin when he suddenly materialised by her side.

'Oh, Lord! You…you gave me a fright,' she gasped, peering at his shadowy figure in the dim light. 'I…I haven't thanked you for changing my bedroom. I'm really…er…really very grateful.'

But Ace didn't seem particularly interested in discussing her change of accommodation.

'It was nothing,' he said, with a dismissive wave of his hand, 'I'm far more interested in the fact that it's time you and I had a long talk.'

'Yes, well…unfortunately, I'm feeling very tired just at the moment…' she muttered nervously. 'Maybe tomorrow…?'

'I don't think so.' He gave a low, sardonic laugh. 'There are one or two items we need to get sorted out straight away. Such as, whatever happened to "Eloise"…?' he added, with another low rumble of laughter.

'Forget her!' Lois told him breathlessly, desperately searching for an avenue of escape from the tall, dominant figure looming over her in the dark hall. 'She never existed beyond my eighteenth birthday, in any case. So, please forget her—now and for ever!'

'Believe me—I've tried! But, unfortunately, for some strange reason I can't seem to get her out of my mind,' he murmured, and she shivered at the deep, disturbing note of sensuality in his voice as he moved closer to her trembling body.

Despite its large space, the tension in the dimly lit hall now felt so thick and claustrophobic she could almost cut it with a knife, Lois thought hysterically. Her mouth was dry with fear and apprehension. Her heart seemed to be pounding and thumping like a sledgehammer, a rip-tide of sexual response racing through her veins as he clasped hold of her arm, and she could feel the touch of his long, muscular thigh against her own.

'Go away! Leave…leave me alone!' she croaked huskily, summoning all her dwindling reserves of strength as she twisted away from his grip, before swiftly spinning around on her heels and bolting up the broad staircase.

'It's no good running away from me,' Ace called after her fast disappearing figure. 'We're going to have to talk sooner or later, you know.'

Not if I've got anything to do with it! Lois promised herself grimly, desperately trying to remember the way back to her room as she sped down one long, dark corridor after another.

CHAPTER FOUR

EVENTUALLY, more by luck than judgement, Lois finally managed to reach the sanctuary of her bedroom.

Quickly discarding her clothes, she made her way into the bathroom and turned on the shower, almost groaning with pleasure as the warmth and comfort of the hot water gently soothed her tired body.

Had it been one hell of a day—or what? she asked herself wearily, realising that, much as she might hate the prospect, she now had no option but to have a long talk with Ace.

In fact, it had obviously been a totally crazy idea to think that she could somehow manage to evade any contact with him. Even if Ace was willing to forget their past encounter—and he had, unfortunately, just made it *very* clear that he wasn't!—she was going to find it impossible to avoid him altogether during the next six weeks. So, she had no alternative. She was going to have to take the bull by the horns, and swear him to secrecy about their brief encounter three months ago.

It wasn't going to be easy, of course. Especially as Lois knew she was going to have to come up with a really good, valid reason why Ace must never divulge their previous meeting. And that wasn't all. She was *also* going to need a good explanation of why she needed to ensure his silence as far as Emily was concerned, as well.

Obviously no parent liked to hear criticism of their child. But, unfortunately, while his daughter was clearly an engaging and interesting girl, it was equally clear that she was also a hopelessly incorrigible chatterbox. Lois shivered at the thought of just how easily the youngster, with one or two careless remarks, could so quickly manage to torpedo this film.

On top of which...there was also the question of Emily's mother. It was obviously vitally important that Ace's wife was kept in the dark, too.

'O what a tangled web we weave, when first we practise to deceive...'

Lois grimaced at the truth of the old saying. A 'tangled web' was the perfect description for the predicament in which she now found herself. In fact, just trying to think of all the various ramifications was enough to give her a bad headache. If she didn't watch out, she'd probably forget which particular version of events she'd told to whom! Still, it was her own stupid fault for getting into this mess—and she'd just have to somehow dig herself out of it.

Quite apart from anything else, she certainly had no intention of causing any problems in Ace's marriage. It was obviously important for them both to realise that their romantic encounter on that lovely Philippine island had been merely a brief, totally regrettable incident, and one which *must* be buried and forgotten as swiftly as possible. The fact that she found herself insanely attracted to Ace's tall, dark handsome figure, was clearly yet another problem which she was going to have to sort out for herself.

Turning off the shower and wrapping her slim figure in a warm, fluffy towel, Lois plugged in her hairdryer and began to blow-dry her long, curly red hair.

Dismayed to note that her hands were still trembling slightly with nervous tension, she made a determined effort to pull herself together. After all, she was a successful actress, right? So, she shouldn't have any problem convincing everyone that Ace was a complete stranger. Or treating both he and his daughter—not to mention his wife and the rest of the film crew—in a perfectly normal and friendly manner.

Switching off the dryer, and vigorously brushing the tangles from her hair, Lois tried to concentrate on coming up with an explanation which would satisfy Ace. Maybe she could capitalise on his ignorance of the film business? Would he swallow the idea that because of her star status she must appear as pure as the driven snow…? And, thus, even a whisper about their previous liaison could seriously damage her reputation…?

It might work, she told herself, putting down her brush and slipping into a thin, ivory silk dressing gown. In any case, it was certainly worth a try. Feeling a lot more cheerful, she opened the door and walked slowly back into the bedroom.

A fraction of a second later, she stiffened like a wary animal, her slim figure rigid and tense with an intuitive feeling of impending danger.

'Danger' is exactly the right word! was the first thought to flash through her brain as in the pale, warm glow of the bedside lights she spied Ace's tall, rangy figure lounging at his ease in one of the blue armchairs.

'How in the hell did you get in here?' she demanded angrily.

'Well, it wasn't very difficult,' he drawled, his voice heavy with sardonic amusement. 'I merely walked up the corridor and opened your door.'

'Well, you can open it again—and walk right back *down* the corridor!' she informed him bluntly. 'Besides, this is *my* bedroom, and you've no right to be here. None at all!'

'Oh, I don't know about that…' he murmured mockingly, making absolutely no attempt to comply with her request. 'After all, this *is* my house—and you wouldn't be here if I hadn't rescued you from that monstrous State Bedroom.'

'OK...OK, I've already said that I'm very grateful,' Lois snapped, before suddenly becoming conscious not only of being stark naked beneath her dressing gown, but also of her bare feet and the tangled cloud of newly washed hair flowing down over her shoulders.

'All right...let's cut the cackle—and get down to brass tacks,' she continued breathlessly, painfully aware of the nervous quake in her voice. 'What do you want?'

Ace laughed. 'Oh, come on, Lois! That *has* to be one of the most stupid questions I've ever heard. Surely it must be obvious...' He paused, his gleaming grey eyes beneath their heavy lids moving slowly down over her slim figure, clothed only in the thin silk gown. 'Well, let's put it this way: even a raving idiot should be able to work out *exactly* what I want!'

'In your dreams, buddy!' she retorted fiercely, her cheeks flushing with anger.

How *dared* he mentally undress her—a well-established Hollywood star, for heaven's sake!—in such a crude, disgusting manner? Did he think she was some floozy starlet, who might be prepared to put up with such nonsense? Because, if so, he was *very* much mistaken!

'Believe me,' she continued grimly, 'whatever idea you may have in that nasty mind of yours—you're definitely *not* getting it!'

However, if she'd hoped that her blunt rebuttal would put him sharply in his place, Lois realised that nothing—other than possibly an atomic explosion—was going to shift this man from the room. Or put him out of countenance in any way.

'Actually,' he drawled smoothly, stretching out his legs and leaning back in the chair, 'I'm quite old enough to know that what I want and what I can get are two quite different things. So, in the meantime, why don't we settle for a good long talk?'

Lois wrapped her arms nervously about her figure, glaring down at the man lounging so casually in the armchair.

Despite the fact that it was a large room, it seemed filled to overflowing with his dominant presence. Beneath the slim-fitting dark trousers and the soft, pale lovat-green cashmere sweater over a casual white shirt, unbuttoned at the neck to display his strongly tanned throat, Ace's lean, tautly muscled frame seemed to ooze with an overwhelming impression of power and confidence. There was clearly very little which escaped those glinting grey eyes beneath their heavy lids. And his air of relaxed, sensual charm was already badly effecting her pulse-rate.

For heaven's sakes! What was wrong with her? She'd come across plenty of really attractive, sexy guys. So, why should *this* man have the ability to make her toes curl? To cause her to become breathless with desire and tremble like jello just as soon as she laid eyes on his handsome face…?

He should carry a government health warning, she told herself grimly. Something along the lines of: 'Watch out—this man is highly dangerous!' would just about hit the mark.

Taking a deep breath, Lois made a determined effort to get a grip on the situation.

'You're quite right,' she told him as calmly as she could. 'We *do* need to talk. But this is neither the right time nor the right place for such a discussion,' she added firmly, walking over to her dressing table and turning her back on him as she fiddled nervously with some of her jewellery. 'So, if you'll just let yourself out, I suggest that we both try and forget this regrettable incident.'

'Regrettable incident...?' He gave a dry bark of sardonic laughter. '*What incident*? My dear girl—I haven't even laid a finger on you!'

'Yes...well...you're not going to, either,' she snapped, painfully aware of the rising note of panic in her voice—and equally aware that she was behaving like a total birdbrain.

What had happened to the sophisticated actress who could normally cope with guys like Ace with one hand tied behind her back—while also tap-dancing and whistling the Star Spangled Banner? How come she was now acting more like a nervous, pathetically feeble sixteen-year-old?

'Look,' she said at last, continuing to keep her back to him, 'it's been a long day, and I really *am* very tired. I realise we've got a lot to talk about. But surely it can wait until tomorrow?

'I'm not trying to put you off with some lame excuse,' she continued as Ace remained ominously silent. 'But you must see that we're going to need some time to discuss what to do about...er...about our previous meeting. Not to mention a whole lot of other problems—such as your wife, and—'

'My *wife*?' he exclaimed in a startled, harsh voice as he rose swiftly to his feet. 'What in the hell are you talking about?'

'There's no point in trying to deny the fact that you're a married man,' she retorted, raising her chin defiantly as she turned around to face him. 'Because I happen to know the truth!'

'Oh, really?' he drawled with grim, silky menace as he began moving slowly across the carpet towards her.

'I...I'm not sitting in moral judgement, here. Because

we both…I mean…what happened on that island was…well, it was as much my fault as yours,' she assured him hurriedly, backing nervously away from his tall, clearly angry figure.

'If you're saying it takes two to tango, you're damn right—it does!' he grated.

'OK…OK…I'm willing to admit that it was probably all *my* fault—if it makes you feel any happier,' she snapped, bitterly aware of the hot colour flooding over her cheeks. 'But the fact remains that I have, as you know, already met your daughter. And Emily has made several references to her mother. Therefore, it's perfectly clear to me that you…'

Her voice died away as he suddenly gave a loud bark of harsh, caustic laugher.

'Don't give up the day job, Lois!' he drawled in a hard, crushing tone of voice. 'Because anyone who can add two and two—and come up with God knows *what* wrong number, is definitely *no* mathematician!'

'I…I don't know what you mean…'

'Well, now…' he murmured, the anger swiftly draining from his tense, rigid body as he stared intently down at her nervous, trembling figure, his mouth twitching in silent humour as he noted the deep crimson flush covering her pale face.

'Yes, I freely admit that I *was* married, a long time ago—to a woman called Martina. And Emily is indeed our daughter. However, my sweet idiot, Martina and I have been divorced for many years. And, although I'll also admit to having been involved with various women in the past, I can assure you that there is no one else in my life at the moment.

'Well…that's not *strictly* true, of course,' he continued, drawing her trembling figure into his arms. 'Ever since meeting a certain lady called Eloise, some three months ago, I've unfortunately been unable to think about anyone else. And I've been rather hoping that she might feel exactly the same way...'

'No...absolutely not...' Lois muttered helplessly, her tired mind trying to absorb the fact that Ace *wasn't* married after all.

She also seemed unable to find the strength to pull herself away from his embrace. In fact, although she could hardly bear to acknowledge the truth, it was nothing short of bliss to be able to rest her aching head against his shoulder and to feel his strong arms closing about her weary, exhausted figure.

'I'm very sorry to hear that,' he murmured huskily, raising a hand to gently tuck a lock of hair behind her ear. 'Because, strange as it may seem, I fear that she seems to have captured my heart.

'Still...there you go. That's life, I suppose,' he continued, grinning down at the girl, whose head was buried in the curve of his shoulder, clearly quite content to remain nestled in his arms. 'Off with the old...and on with the new—that's what I always say. So, it's now clearly a case of "Goodbye, Eloise" and "Hello, Lois!" Right?'

'No—of course it's not right!' she muttered crossly against his sweater, trying to keep a straight face as she felt his broad chest shaking with suppressed laughter.

'Now, *just* a minute!' he protested, clasping hold of her slim shoulders and holding her away from him as he smiled down into her wide, troubled blue eyes. 'You can't *both* be turning me down. It's simply not fair! Surely one of you ought to take pity on a poor, lonely man? God knows, I don't ask for much. Just an occasional kind word, a few crumbs of comfort after a hard day's work...'

'Oh—*shut up*!' she retorted, a reluctant grin on her lips as he gave an infectious rumble of laughter. 'And, don't even *think* of giving up your day job, Ace,' she added caustically. 'Because that performance of yours was nothing but pure *ham*!'

'Oh, dear. You mean there's no chance of me getting a part in this film you're making?'

Lois gave a snort of wry amusement. 'About as much chance as I have of becoming Lady of the Manor! So, I think we'd better just stick to our own professions, don't you? Now...if you'll just be serious, for a moment,' she added sternly, 'I'm quite willing to have a long talk tomorrow. We can discuss—'

'Tomorrow is another day. I'm chiefly interested in the here and now. And don't make the mistake of thinking that I'm not being very serious. Or that I'm fooling around,' he told her firmly, the laughter dying on his face as his expression became hard and determined. 'Because, you can be *my* Lady of the Manor—any day you please.'

Startled by the flat, hard note of sincerity in his voice, Lois wondered if she had quite understood the meaning behind his words. Surely...surely this man couldn't have just...well, sort of...asked her to marry him? No, of course he hadn't, she told herself firmly. She must be far more tired than she'd realised. Which was all the more reason for him to leave the room, and for her to hit the sack, as soon as possible.

But, unfortunately, while she'd been mentally trying to get her act together, Ace had clearly been interested in quite another scenario.

'No...' she muttered, desperately trying to control her wayward mind as she felt his hands moving slowly down over her spine. 'You really must go...I mean...it's so late. It's clearly time we both went to bed,' she added wildly, gasping at the warm, erotic touch of his fingers sliding sinuously over the thin silk gown.

'That's the best idea you've had all night,' he drawled, the gleam in his grey eyes and his explicit touch as he gently caressed the firm curves of her body causing a rising tide of desire to flood through her trembling figure.

'Please…please don't do this, Ace,' she begged huskily, struggling in vain to tear her eyes away from the intense, searching, almost hypnotic gleam in his glinting grey eyes.

The silence lengthened between them in the still, quiet room, the tension mounting with each passing second, until she could almost feel it hammering in her head. She couldn't move…she couldn't say or do anything. Her body felt as if it was burning with a fiery heat, shaken by frenzied shivers of excitement running riot through every fibre of her being.

Slowly and deliberately, he lowered his dark head, her nerves almost at screaming point by the time his lips gently touched her own. She was acutely conscious of the musky scent of his cologne, the faint flush of arousal beneath the tanned skin of his high cheekbones, and the strength of the hand sweeping up to hold her head firmly beneath him while the other closed tightly about her waist, drawing her closer to the hard, male contours of his body. She could feel a fierce clenching of erotic desire in the pit of her stomach as his kiss deepened, inciting the same passion and hunger she'd felt in his arms all those months ago.

Feeling as though she was drowning in a vortex of physical sensations, she wound her arms about his neck, her fingers burying themselves in his thick, dark hair as she feverishly responded to the increasing urgency of his embrace. However foolish and ill-advised this might be, she was aware only of a deep need, an overwhelming desire so fierce and intense that it completely obliterated all sense and caution.

Totally swept up in a whirlwind of overriding lust and passion, she merely gave a slight groan of disappointment when his lips left hers for a moment as he carried her swiftly over to the bed. Lowering her down against the pillows, he slipped his hands sensually over her soft silk gown as he caressed her soft curves with an increasingly hungry, ardent passion which left her dazed and trembling in his arms,

'Oh, my darling…!' he groaned, burying his face in the fragrant cloud of her hair for a moment, before untying the belt of her gown and exposing her body to his view. She shivered with delight, and a low, husky moan broke from her throat as his hands moved erotically over her bare flesh, before rising to cup her breasts, his fingers softly caressing the hard, swollen points with a slow, sensual movement which caused her senses to spin completely out of control.

She barely heard his soft murmurs of endearment, totally submerged in a sea of delicious sensations as his lovemaking became more intense. Shivering with delight beneath the sweet seduction of his mouth and hands on her soft flesh, it was only when she caught his thickly whispered, 'Such wonderful breasts…so much larger than I remember…' that reality began to break through the mist of passion.

'Oh…no! We can't…I mustn't…' Lois muttered helplessly, suddenly realising that she'd forgotten all about the fact that she was expecting a baby. She had no idea if it was possible…she'd never thought to ask the Harley Street doctor about whether lovemaking would harm the child in her womb.

'Darling—relax!' he murmured softly. 'We're neither of us married. We're both as free as birds and hurting no one. So…'

'No! You don't understand…' she moaned, knowing

that she couldn't possibly tell him the truth, but not knowing what else to do. 'I'm not…not strong…we really can't…'

'There's no need to worry…I'll be very gentle,' he promised, preventing her from saying anything more as he possessed her lips in a warm kiss of such sweet tenderness that she was completely lost. Trapped within the fierce grip of a primitive force quite beyond her control, and slipping helplessly down below waves of pulsating passion, she dimly realised that, as he'd assured her, Ace was tempering the urgency of his own desire, controlling the force of his passion as he gently and tenderly led her from one exquisite delight to another. Until he at last brought them both to a soaring high peak of mutual ecstasy.

Lois gave a heavy sigh, leaning back against the wall, and massaging the tired muscles at the back of her neck.

Although she ought to be used to the long delays involved with film-making by now, it had also been an equally long day—ever since she'd been awoken at first light to attend Make-up. And, having had her hair piled up on top of her head—along with a crazy confection of ribbons, feathers and goodness knows what else attached to the mass of curls on her crown—there was no way she could gain any rest by lying down.

They had now been shooting this film for a week, and it seemed as if she was *still* walking on eggshells as far as her own personal life was concerned.

Drowsily replete after their lovemaking the night of her arrival at Ratcliffe Hall, Lois had drifted off to sleep within the safety and comfort of Ace's arms. But when her alarm call had woken her at six o'clock the next morning she had found him gone. Only the rumpled bedclothes and a fresh red rose lying on the pillow beside her had given any hint of his presence in her room the previous night.

Unfortunately, deliriously happy and fulfilling as their lovemaking had been, it had solved precisely nothing.

They still hadn't had an opportunity to have a really good, long talk, since the shooting schedule had involved not only the necessity of her being on set for most of the day, but had also included many night scenes as well. And, although she might have had the burden of actual adultery lifted from her shoulders, the situation was still as fraught as ever.

Quite apart from needing to secure his silence regarding their meeting in the Philippines, Lois now knew that in allowing Ace to make love to her last week she had disastrously compounded an already tense and difficult problem.

If she had hoped that their first meeting had been merely an isolated, regrettable incident—and that she could easily forget that it had ever happened—she now knew that she'd been quite wrong. Unfortunately, it was only too evident that she was desperately vulnerable to Ace's dark attraction. The way she had succumbed so quickly and so completely to his lovemaking merely demonstrated how susceptible she was: totally weak and defenceless against the sheer power of his overwhelming sensual appeal. And he didn't even have to touch her! It was enough for him to be merely standing beside her...

Lois gave a heavy sigh, trying to ignore the quick spasm of excitement which flared through her body whenever she thought about Ace, a longing and a need so intense that no amount of cool reason and hard sense could dispel it.

The plain fact was whenever she was anywhere near him she seemed to lose any power of judgement and logic. So, how she was going to cope for the remaining five weeks of this film, she had absolutely no idea.

But that wasn't her only problem, right?

What was complicating matters at the moment was the fact that, as Peggy Fraser had so accurately pointed out, her figure was now definitely beginning to change shape. Luckily, these Regency gowns, with their waists fixed high under the bosom, might have been designed specifically for pregnant ladies! But her breast measurement seemed to be rapidly increasing, and it was beginning to look as if she could wave goodbye to her waist as well.

All of which meant that however great the temptation, she must definitely *not*, under *any* circumstances, allow Ace to make love to her again. After all, the guy clearly wasn't a fool. And since he must have gone through his wife's pregnancy, before she gave birth to Emily, Lois knew that she couldn't take the risk of him getting a glimpse of her rapidly changing figure.

With another heavy sigh, she turned to look out of one of the tall floor-to-ceiling windows of the large dining room. It seemed a crying shame to be cooped up inside on such a lovely, warm summer's day, she thought, gazing longingly out at the rolling green pastures of the parkland surrounding Ratcliffe Hall. What she wouldn't give to be able to enjoy the fresh sunshine—instead of being cooped up in this dark, if magnificent room, with the light from massive Venetian chandeliers glinting down on a huge mahogany table covered with sparkling crystal glasses and heavy silver cutlery.

So many scenes of Regency life seemed to be concerned with wining and dining, Lois told herself wryly, watching idly as the director and the chief cameraman conferred in a corner of the room, working out their shots for the next scene. In fact, not only had they been filming one gargantuan meal after another—but there were four or five scenes still to be shot in this room. Which meant, alas, that she was going to have to put up with more days of feeling queasy at the sight and smell of so much food.

However, if she hadn't been feeling slightly sick for most of the time, Lois knew that she would have enjoyed working with so many fine actors. Her leading man, Neil Gray, was proving to be an absolute rock. Especially when they'd both had to cope with a bad attack of 'first-night nerves' from the young actress playing Lois' daughter in the film.

A young eighteen-year-old, and fresh out of drama school, the poor girl had completely lost her cool. But after being comforted by Neil she'd gamely pulled herself together and was now shaping up nicely.

Actually, Lois reminded herself with a grin, the young actress's quick recovery from her collapse had probably been due more to Emily's intervention in the crisis rather than anything Neil had said. Because, amidst all the hoo-ha of raving hysterics, it had been Emily's cry of, 'What a stupid girl! Let *me* have a go. I won't be sloppy and collapse with hysterics!' which had swiftly persuaded the young actress to dry her tears, quickly pulling herself together at the threat of losing her job.

However, Emily's attempt to become a film star overnight had given Lois an idea.

While the film crew had become fond of Ace's daughter, there was no doubt that her incessant chatter meant that she could, at times, be a flaming nuisance. However, after Lois had a word with the director, he'd laughed, before agreeing to her suggestion that he might use the young girl as one of the young servants in the below-stairs kitchen scenes.

This offer of a part had succeeded in keeping Emily as quiet as a mouse for the last three days. And had also done much to approve her appearance.

'I don't see why I've got to remove my nose ring,' the young girl had grumbled. 'It's sort of "me", if you know what I mean…'

'Yes, well, maybe it's time for a change of image?' Lois had told her. 'In any case, if you'd studied a bit harder at school, you'd realise that people in Regency times didn't believe in trying to make themselves as ugly as possible,' she'd added coolly.

'Yes, but…'

'Domestic servants in those days were far too busy struggling to keep body and soul together to have time to waste on being a rebellious teenager,' Lois had stated bluntly. 'So, if you want the part, kid—that ring has to go!'

'Oh—all right!' Emily had muttered, caving in at the prospect of losing her moment of glory, and had even— to everyone's astonishment—meekly allowed the hairdresser to cut her hair into a more graceful bob.

If she'd wanted a pat on the back for improving Emily's appearance—and of course she didn't—she would have been rewarded by Ace, smiling gratefully across the room at dinner last night, when listening to his daughter's excited explanations of how she was now a 'real live actress'.

Immersed in her thoughts, Lois was dragged back to the present by a commotion from the other side of the room. Turning her head, she saw standing in the open doorway of the dining room a tall, slim and remarkably pretty blonde woman, possibly slightly older than herself, who was regarding the scene before her with a wide, beaming smile.

'Darling—what *fun!*' the blonde woman cried, waving her arms with excitement.

As Lois' gaze sharpened, she saw Ace emerging from the darkness of the hall to join the woman, his tall figure looking stiff and distinctly uncomfortable.

'Come away, Martina,' Ace growled. 'Everyone has quite enough work to do without you getting in the way,' he added, clasping hold of the woman's arm and clearly trying to lead her away.

'Honestly, darling! There's no need to be *quite* so stuffy. After all, this is *my* sort of world, isn't it? I mean…I know all about cameras and sets and that sort of thing,' she protested, clearly refusing to budge an inch as she continued to look about her with interest. 'I expect I could even give these people some advice, if they asked for it.'

'Who's the poisonous bitch in the doorway?' Neil Gray enquired, strolling over to join Lois and raising one dark, quizzical eyebrow as he gazed at the couple across the room.

Turning to give him a slight smile, Lois thought that Neil was looking remarkably handsome in his costume. With his broad shoulders encased in a royal blue velvet tail coat over a pale gold embroidered waistcoat, he looked every bit the nineteenth-century gentleman, his high, stiff-collared shirt and snowy white lacy cravat throwing into strong contrast his swarthy good looks and black curly hair. In fact, with his tautly muscled lower limbs encased in pale gold pantaloons and white stockings, ending in patent leather pumps with wide gold buckles, she thought her young leading man looked pretty nifty. And definitely capable of causing his many female fans to swoon with delight.

Dave Green, the producer, might have been right when he'd intimated on the day of her arrival that, in real life, Neil lacked both the commanding presence and rampant sex appeal possessed in abundance by Ace. Nevertheless, he had considerable acting ability. And, since he was also highly photogenic, his handsome face and figure had rapidly promoted him to 'matinee idol' status with a host of devoted fans.

Luckily, it seemed that Neil clearly admired Lois' looks, *and* her own acting ability, which meant they'd both got on like a house on fire from day one. All of which was contributing towards a very happy and harmonious working relationship.

'I'm starving,' Neil complained. 'It's time we got this scene wrapped up and in the can. Which we certainly ought to have done by now,' he added irritably. 'Why hasn't someone told that damned woman to get off the set?'

'Well…' Lois shrugged. 'I rather think…in fact, I'm almost sure it must be Lord Ratcliffe's ex-wife,' she murmured, dismayed to find herself feeling a sharp, sudden pang as the blonde woman lifted a beautifully manicured hand to gently pat Ace's face.

'Do relax, darling!' Martina laughed. 'You never know. They might actually give me a part in this film!'

'Over my dead body!' Neil snorted.

My sentiments exactly, Lois agreed silently, instinctively deciding that she definitely didn't like the woman standing across the room.

It was nothing to do with the fact that she was undoubtedly Ace's ex-wife, either. Absolutely not. It was simply that…well, if there was one thing she *really* hated, it was empty-headed flibbetigibbet blondes. Especially those who didn't have the sense to realise that everyone in this room was busily engaged in trying to get ready for the next scene. And that the very last thing they needed was some idiot woman getting in the way.

Whether Ace had picked up the vibes from the impatient film crew, or whether his own good sense had finally led him to take some firm action, Lois couldn't tell. But, clearly deciding that enough was enough, he firmly gripped the woman's arm, grimly ignoring her violent protests as he dragged her from the room.

It would be nice to think that that was the end of the matter, Lois told herself as she and the other members of the cast took their places, ready for the shooting of the next scene. Unfortunately, she had a very strong feeling that she had definitely *not* seen the last of Martina.

CHAPTER FIVE

IT WAS a wonderfully warm summer's day, Lois thought, walking slowly through the park towards a small building surrounded by tress some distance away.

Although it was now mid-morning, the long grass was still slightly damp with dew; a fragrant light breeze rustled the leaves of a nearby clump of tall oaks, and the hum of a tractor working in an adjacent field was the only sound to disturb the still, peaceful scene.

The director, Peter Danvers, would have to do something about *that*, she told herself with a grin, raising a hand to shield her eyes against the bright sunshine as she turned to view the hive of activity on the other side of the park. He certainly couldn't afford to have the sound of noisy, modern-day machinery as a background to his filming of a rural, nineteenth-century hay-making scene which, as Peggy had forecast, he'd decided to incorporate into the film at the last minute.

But the director's problems were, thankfully, nothing to do with her. For the first time in their tight schedule she'd been allowed a whole day off. Well…at least until later this afternoon. So, she could only wish Peter the very best of luck as he tried to control all those men with their heavy, dangerous-looking scythes—while she played hooky!

Determined to enjoy her first real chance to be out in the open air, Lois had slipped on a simple, loose sleeveless silk dress in her favourite shade of aquamarine blue, before helping herself to some apples and a small bottle of mineral water from the kitchen. Placing them in a light knapsack, together with her dark glasses and some sun cream, she'd quietly left the house. And now, knapsack slung over her shoulder, her soft mohair rug in one hand and a book in the other, she was looking forward to a day's uninterrupted peace and quiet.

In fact, it had taken some ingenuity on her part to avoid having Emily join her. Much as she liked the young girl, Ace's daughter seemed to be firmly in the grip of a bad case of hero worship at the moment. And, although she didn't want to be too unkind, it was proving a relief to escape the incessant chatter of the youngster, who'd seemed to dog her footsteps from morning to night over the past three weeks.

On the other hand…Emily's constant presence had meant that she'd been able to avoid being left on her own with Ace. Although that hardly explained why he'd seemed so tight-lipped and bad-tempered during the past few days. For instance, there had been absolutely no reason—after she and Neil had finished rehearsing a scene together yesterday—for Ace to stalk past them, calling out sarcastically over his shoulder, 'I hope you two *lovely* people are thoroughly enjoying yourselves!'

Not only had it been an embarrassing situation, but it had left both Neil and herself totally mystified as to how they'd managed to upset their host. In fact, if Lois hadn't been so determined to keep well out of Ace's way, she'd have stormed straight into his study and told him *exactly* what she thought about his quite unnecessary rude behaviour!

On the other hand, maybe it was unfair to blame the guy too much, for being so tetchy? Because he was clearly bending under the strain and burden of not only having to deal with his rebellious adolescent daughter—but also with an extremely difficult ex-wife.

However, to be honest, there was no escaping the fact

that Martina Ratcliffe was a very beautiful woman. And she was quite capable, when it suited her, of turning on an amazing amount of charm. Unfortunately, she also appeared to have the hide of an elephant—totally impervious to anything other than her own wishes and desires. And for some strange reason she seemed determined to stay at Ratcliffe Hall, digging in her heels and refusing to listen to any heavy hints, from both the producer and director of the film, when they suggested that she might like to return to the bright lights of London.

'Oh, no,' she'd murmured, shaking her blonde head and widening her goo-goo green eyes while coming up with one feeble excuse after another. The latest had been that she must act as chaperon to 'Dear Emily—so nervous and such a delicate little girl.' A statement which had been greeted with hilarity by members of the film crew, who'd by now clearly come to the conclusion that 'dear Emily' was as tough as old boots.

At first Lois had assumed that Martina was merely as starstruck as her daughter. But now she wasn't quite so sure. The blonde woman was, of course, still making a thorough-going nuisance of herself. But she appeared to have given up the idea of actually appearing in the film. And for the last few days they'd been spared her freely expressed view on how to shoot any particular scene. So, why was she still hanging around Ratcliffe Hall?

The only scenario Lois could come up with was the idea that Martina and Ace might be intending to get back together again. Martina certainly appeared to be very fond of her ex-husband. Indeed, whenever she'd seen the couple over the past two weeks, Ace had seemed to have his ex-wife glued firmly to his side.

So, maybe it was just as well that she and Ace hadn't seen too much of each other, Lois told herself heavily, feeling depressed as she walked slowly across the grass

towards the small building—which looked like a minia-
ture Greek temple. Because if there was the slightest
chance of a reconciliation between Martina and her ex-
husband it would be quite wrong of her to do anything
other than to keep well out of their way.

After a quick inspection of the 'temple', which turned
out to be composed of merely one large and rather dusty
room, containing some elegant wrought-iron chairs, Lois
decided that she'd prefer to be outside, in the sunshine.
Putting on her dark glasses and spreading her rug over
the wide stone steps, she settled down to read her book.

On exploring the huge old library, which seemed filled
to overflowing with ancient leather-bound volumes, Lois
had come across *Mansfield Park*. It was her favourite
amongst Jane Austen's novels. Although she hadn't read
it for some time, she was looking forward to renewing
her acquaintance with the heroine who, like herself, had
come as a stranger to live in large country house very
similar to Ratcliffe Hall.

Totally absorbed in her book, Lois had no idea of how
much time had passed when she was suddenly startled
to hear the sharp crack of a twig. Abruptly raising her
head, she saw Ace advancing over the grass towards her.

That's all I need just at the moment, she thought
glumly, ruthlessly suppressing the fleeting tremor of excitement which had rippled through her body at the sight
of his tall, rangy figure. Casually dressed in a slim pair
of denims and a short-sleeved, thin blue cotton shirt, Ace
was, as usual, looking devastatingly attractive.

If those jeans were any tighter, he wouldn't be able
to get them on over his feet, Lois told herself grimly,
viewing him from behind the safe darkness of her sunglasses. And as for that open-necked shirt, clinging like
glue to his broad shoulders and firm torso—it was nothing but a disgrace! In fact, it was definitely about time

that someone brought in a law preventing sexy guys like Ace from wearing clothes designed to raise the blood pressure of poor, susceptible females!

'I'm here to deliver your lunch,' he informed her as she continued to regard him in silence.

'In fact,' he continued with a grin, 'I'm here on the express orders of Nora. I believe you've already met my old nanny?' he added as she blinked in confusion.

'Oh, yes...yes, I have. She seems a real treasure,' Lois murmured, quickly recalling her meeting with the elderly woman.

Although she hadn't seen very much of the housekeeper, it was undoubtedly Nora who'd made sure that her room was always filled with fresh flowers, and a bowl of fruit set temptingly on one of the side-tables in her bedroom.

'Treasure or not, Nora has very firmly laid down the law. To quote her own words: "That girl isn't eating enough to keep a sparrow alive." So...' He shrugged. 'I'm merely doing as I'm told. Which is to deliver this hamper,' he added, placing a wicker basket on the step beside her. 'And to see that you consume its contents.'

'But I'm not at all hungry,' she protested. 'I've got some apples, and—'

'Hold it!' He grinned, coming over to sit down beside her. 'Even if you don't want to hear the message there's no point in arguing with the messenger. If you *really* hate the idea of smoked salmon sandwiches and a nice, cold jug of freshly made lemonade—I suggest you take it up with Nora.

'For my part,' he continued in a smooth drawl, stretching out his long legs and leaning back on his elbows to gaze up at the clear blue sky above, 'I wouldn't *dream* of disagreeing with my old nanny. Quite frankly, Lois, I'm far too much of a coward! The old bat used

to rule both my brother and myself with a rod of iron—
and nothing seems to have changed since she became
my housekeeper.'

Lois smiled as, despite his hard words, she registered
the warm, tender note in Ace's voice as he spoke about
the elderly woman.

'Do you have many brothers and sisters?' she enquired idly, as he began unpacking the wicker hamper.
'Your house is so large. It seems designed for a whole
tribe of children.'

'No, there was only Mark and myself, but we weren't
brought up here, of course,' he said, explaining that his
father, as a younger son, had been left to forge his own
path in life while his uncle Hector had inherited both
Ratcliffe Hall and its estate.

'That's the way things happen here in England. It's
called "primogeniture"—which, freely translated,
means the eldest son inherits the title and the whole estate. I can't justify the system. In fact, I think it's a rather
barbaric custom—and definitely one which discriminates
against women,' he added, pouring her a glass of icy-
cold lemonade.

'However, the only thing to be said in its favour is
that it has, over past generations, prevented large estates
from being broken up—and thus preserved much of the
countryside from becoming one large housing estate.
Unlike the custom in France—where even small farms
are required, by law, to be split evenly between any children of a marriage—the whole of an English estate is
customarily passed on intact from eldest son to eldest
son.'

Lois frowned. 'OK…I get the idea. But don't women
ever inherit a title?' she asked as he handed her some
sandwiches.

'No.' He shook his dark head. 'While there *are* some

rare exceptions, of course, a title can normally only be claimed by the next direct male descendant. Which is exactly how, and why, I found myself landed with a huge old house and this rundown estate just a few months ago.'

Listening as Ace proceeded to relate the long, sad tale which had led to his inheritance, she couldn't help but feel that he had taken on quite a burden.

'I must say that is a really very, *very* sad story you've just told me,' she murmured, gazing at him with deep sympathy. 'And it must have been shattering to lose your brother at such a young age. But it does seem a crying shame that Emily can't inherit Ratcliffe Hall.'

Ace shrugged. 'I don't think Emily sees it that way. In fact, if it hadn't been for this film, I'd have had real problems keeping her occupied and happy during her stay here. As far as she is concerned,' he added with a grin, 'the countryside is "dead boring". And, to be honest, I have to admit there is very little here to interest a young teenager.'

'I expect she'll grow to love the place when she's older.'

'She may,' Ace agreed, before turning his head to grin down at the empty picnic basket. 'Well...well! It seems Nora was quite right, after all!'

Following his gaze, Lois was amazed to discover that she'd been so absorbed, listening to the story of his unexpected and unwelcome inheritance, that she didn't seem to have lost her appetite after all.

'OK...I'll freely admit that those sandwiches were quite delicious.' She grinned, surprised to find herself feeling a lot more cheerful and energetic than she had earlier.

Closing the lid of the wicker basket, Ace rose slowly

to his feet, turning to gaze up at the grey stone temple behind them.

'Having fulfilled Nora's instructions to make sure you ate your lunch, this seems a good opportunity to check whether the place is in need of repair. I haven't yet had a good chance to inspect it. Do you want to come and have a look?' he added, putting out a hand to help her to her feet.

'I wonder why someone decided to build this small one-roomed building so far away from the main house?' Lois asked, gazing around the dusty interior some minutes later. 'Was it some kind of summerhouse?'

'It could have been,' he agreed slowly. 'But over two hundred years ago—with a host of servants to attend to a rich man's every whim—it's probably more likely that this type of folly was designed to be used for grand picnics, or some kind of outdoor musical entertainment.'

'That sounds fun. In fact, from all I've heard—and provided you were very wealthy, of course—it was a really great life in those days,' she murmured enviously, walking over to peer out of a small round window at the back of the room.

'And of course,' Ace said, coming over to stand beside her, 'I imagine that it was also used by those of my ancestors wishing to conduct a romantic liaison...well out of sight of prying eyes. What do you think? Hmm...?'

The softly voiced question seemed to hang heavily in the air, the atmosphere within the dimly lit room becoming all at once highly charged with an unmistakable sexual tension. Lois' mouth felt suddenly dry, the blood pounding in her veins as she found herself swept by an overpowering, crazy urge to turn and throw herself into his arms. Oh, Lord—it was a really bad, *bad* idea to let him show me around this place, she thought, desperately trying to pull her weak, emotional self together.

'I really don't have any thoughts on the matter. In fact, it's time I was getting back to the house,' she said at last, marvelling at the fact that she was somehow managing to sound so calm and steady as she turned to move past him towards the arched entrance of the stone temple.

'No, I don't think so,' he drawled mockingly, catching hold of her arm and spinning her around to face him. 'I'm perfectly well aware that you've done your best to avoid me over the past three weeks,' he added, removing her sunglasses and tossing them down onto a nearby chair as he pulled her reluctant, trembling figure towards him.

'Please! We're filming this afternoon. I...I really do have to go...' she protested huskily.

'Oh, no, you don't! I've had a good look at the schedule. So, I know that you're not on call until early this evening,' he retorted bluntly. 'Or can it be that you can't wait to have yet another so-called "rehearsal" with the glamorous Mr Gray?' he enquired in a harsh, caustic tone of voice.

'What on earth are you talking about?' She gazed up at him with a puzzled frown. 'Surely you can't possibly think that Neil and I...?'

'I don't have to "think",' he ground out savagely. 'It's only too obvious—to anyone with even *half* a brain—that the two of you are thoroughly enjoying those hot, torrid love scenes.'

'I've never heard such nonsense!' she snapped. 'Neil and I have been merely putting on a good performance. Which is *precisely* what we're paid to do. Even with half of *your* stupid brain, you should be able to see that!'

'No wonder you've been keeping well out of my

way!' he continued bitterly, clearly not listening to a word she'd said. 'I can only imagine that trying to cope with two lovers under one roof would tax even a consummate actress like yourself!'

'That's rich—coming from such a two-timing rat!' she lashed back angrily. 'How about you and your ex-wife?'

'What...?'

'Hah—that's stopped you in your tracks, hasn't it? You...you damned Casanova!' she ground out furiously. 'At least Neil and I are only acting. While *you've* obviously been busy performing the real thing!'

'I've never heard anything so ridiculous!' he grated.

'Oh, yeah?' she taunted. 'Tell that to the marines! Because it's clear to everyone what's going on. That stupid woman is all over you like a rash, for heaven's sake!'

Ace stared fiercely down at her in silence for a moment, before giving a low bark of sardonic laughter.

'OK...let's just cool it,' he said in a quieter tone of voice. 'Are you asking me to believe that you and Neil Gray are just putting on an act?'

'Oh—for God's sake!' she muttered with bitter exasperation. '*Of course* that's what we've been doing! As you, yourself, have just said—I really *am* a good actress. And, just in case you're wondering, I certainly did *not* win an Oscar last year by fooling around with my leading man!'

'And you really haven't been making love to the guy?'

'Now, hang on just a minute!' she snapped. 'I'm not prepared to put up with any more of this "third-degree" nonsense. I've already told you about my relationship with Neil—which is *strictly* professional. And that's more than can be said for the way you and your ex-wife have been carrying on!'

'Any "carrying on", as you call it, has been strictly one-sided,' he retorted flatly. 'Martina ran off with a pop star some years ago, and I've had virtually nothing to do with the woman since then—other than any discussions concerning Emily's welfare.'

'So, how come she's always draped all over you like a fur coat?'

Ace shrugged his broad shoulders. 'I have absolutely no idea. Who knows what goes on in that dim mind of hers? All I *can* say, with my hand on my heart, is that since I'm obviously so crazy about you, I totally fail to understand why you should imagine I'd be interested in looking at another woman…?'

Lois stared fixedly at one of the buttons on his shirt. While she'd registered the flat note of sincerity in his voice, concerning his own feelings for her, she still had a very strong suspicion that he was badly underestimating his ex-wife, and her intentions regarding himself. The blonde woman struck her as one very tough lady, perfectly capable of going to extraordinary lengths to get what she wanted. And Lois was quite certain that Martina had her sights very firmly fixed on her ex-husband.

'Well…?' Ace demanded fiercely, his arms closing tightly about her, crushing her breasts against his hard, firm chest.

'OK…OK,' she muttered. 'I'll accept what you say about Martina—if you, in your turn, are prepared to accept that I've absolutely no interest in Neil Gray. Plus the fact that he isn't the slightest bit interested in me. Deal?'

'Yes.' Ace nodded as his lips twisted into a grimace. 'It looks as though I've been a bit of an idiot, doesn't it?'

'I'm not going to argue with that diagnosis,' she informed him bluntly. 'However, while we're on the subject of a deal, this seems a perfect opportunity to mention something else, which is really *vitally* important. I've been trying to find an opportunity to tell you about it, but life—and the damned film schedule—has always seemed to get in the way.'

'All right, I'm listening,' he said. 'But make it short. Because I *do* have some other plans for us this afternoon,' he added with a grin, his arms tightening about her slim figure.

But Lois was hardly listening to his words as she quickly tried to put together a watertight excuse. 'Well, the thing is,' she began slowly, 'I've got a very real problem. And, while I realise that you don't know much about the film industry, I'm going to have to ask you to take my word for the fact that it's a veritable hotbed of crude, brutal gossip. Which is why I'm now asking you—or maybe, begging would be the right word?— never to tell *anyone* about our meeting in the Philippines,' she added, before explaining the various ramifications it could have on her career.

'I really don't see…'

'Believe me, it really *is* important,' she told him urgently. 'If there's even the slightest hint of gossip, Sal Weiser, the main financier behind this film, will be only too happy to pull the rug out from beneath a production which he considered an ''arty-farty'' idea in the first place. And I can't say that I'd be too pleased about seeing myself splashed all over the pages of some low-down film gossip magazine, either,' she added grimly. 'Because they like nothing better than grabbing hold of someone who's successful and pulling them down into the gutter.'

'OK—I've got the picture,' Ace told her. 'So, what do you want me to do?'

Lois hesitated for a moment. 'I'd like you to promise to try and do your best to totally ignore me until this film is wrapped up and in the can.'

'Oh—*come on*!'

'No, please—I'm being serious!' she begged. 'This *really* isn't just some stupid excuse to avoid seeing you. Because you know perfectly well that I...er...I find you very attractive. And I...I believe you feel the same way,' she added, a deep flush rising up over her cheeks. 'But for the next three weeks it really is desperately important that no one gets wind of our...er...our relationship.'

'Let's get this straight. Are you asking me to leave you strictly alone—until you've stopped filming?' he demanded incredulously. And when she nodded, he gave a harsh bark of sardonic laughter.

'That's asking a hell of a lot, isn't it?' he continued in an angry growl. 'However...I'll agree to go along with this crazy scheme of yours. But only one condition. And that is I'm going to insist on seeing you at least once every day, even if only for a quick drink in my private apartment after dinner. Deal?'

There was a long silence while she tried to think the matter through as quickly as possible. But Ace clearly wasn't prepared to give her too much time for prevarication.

Placing a hand under her chin, he raised her face firmly up towards him. 'Well?'

'OK.' She gave a heavy sigh. 'I guess it's a deal.'

However, with his hand still firmly gripping her chin, he stared down searchingly into her blue eyes. 'I wonder...I wonder *why* I have a distinct feeling that there is a great deal more to this request of yours than seems to be apparent at the moment...?'

For several moments he just held her there, imprisoned against him. And, despite all their angry words a few moments ago, she seemed incapable of escape, staring mesmerised up at his mouth and suddenly swept by a fierce ache and longing to feel the hard, sensual lips clasped to her own.

Her heart was beating so fast that her ears seemed filled with its drumming, her senses spinning giddily out of control as she gazed up into his eyes, the intense gleam from beneath the heavy lids causing a flash of hot excitement to zig-zag through her quivering body.

'No! You promised…our deal…let me go!' she gasped, filled with the familiar sick excitement which always possessed her whenever she found herself in this man's arms.

'The deal can damn well wait until tomorrow!' he rasped. 'As for letting you go… Unfortunately I can't seem to do that. Not when your lovely body melts and quivers against mine like this,' he added in a thick, husky voice, before lowering his mouth to brush and tantalise her trembling lips, his hands moving erotically over the silk dress as he sensually caressed her soft curves.

He was right, she thought with despair. There seemed nothing she could do to prevent herself from responding blindly to the demanding possession of his deepening kiss, or the potent urgency of the hard figure pressed so closely to her own. Her breathless pleas for him to stop became an inaudible moan beneath the melting sweetness and soft seduction of his lips.

Just for a few moments she abandoned herself to the overpowering intoxication of his embrace. No one but Ace had ever kissed her like this, so sensually and erotically, demanding that she acknowledge her awareness of her body's needs—and of his. And then, as warning sirens wailed loudly at the back of her brain, and she tried to escape his tight embrace, she discovered that she couldn't, one of his hands having risen to hold her head firmly and immovably beneath him.

Unfortunately, despite knowing that she was acting like an utter fool, her body seemed determined to ignore the danger signals flashing through her mind, instinctively melting against him as she helplessly wound her arms around his neck. She seemed incapable of making any resistance as his fingers moved caressingly over her soft curves, her senses drugged and seduced into acquiescence as he swiftly undid the top buttons of her dress, enabling his lips to slip down over her throat and neck, searching for the firm, warm swell of her breasts.

One moment she was drowning in ecstasy, the next she became aware of Ace cursing violently under his breath as he swiftly let go of her trembling figure. Completely stunned, her legs quivering like jelly, Lois managed to stagger a few feet before collapsing down onto one of the small wrought-iron chairs.

Still helplessly trapped within the thick mist of her own desire, she brushed a distracted, shaking hand through her curly hair as with glazed eyes she saw Ace moving quickly to the doorway.

'*Damn*! That's all I need,' he grated, continuing to swear under his breath as he turned back to face her.

'What…what's wrong?' she asked helplessly, wrapping her slim arms about her trembling body.

However, even as she asked the question Lois could hear a distant voice calling, 'Coo-eee…? Where are you…?'

'Oh, Lord—it's Emily!' she breathed, frantically snatching up her dark sunglasses and trying to do up the top buttons of her dress.

'She'll be here in a moment,' Ace ground out angrily. 'There's no way we can think of trying to hide, either, since she's bound to spot the picnic basket out there on the steps. I love my daughter very much,' he added savagely, 'but just at this moment I could cheerfully wring her damn neck!'

Walking slowly along the corridor to her room, some time later, Lois shuddered as she remembered both her and Ace's hurried attempts to make it look as though they had been merely enjoying a quiet conversation within the Greek temple.

Luckily, Emily had accepted at face value Lois' brief explanation that her colouring and delicate complexion prevented her from staying too long in the sun. And, after all, maybe the girl *had* just arrived in the nick of time? Because it was now abundantly clear that she was quite incapable of putting up any resistance at all to the dark, overwhelming attraction of the girl's father.

Opening the door to her bedroom, she was just thinking that there might be time for her to have a cool, refreshing shower, before reporting to Make-up and Costume for the shoot arranged that evening, when she paused, startled, in the doorway.

'Ah, there you are!'

Blinking foolishly across the room at the sight of Martina, comfortably ensconced in one of the blue armchairs, it was a few seconds before Lois got over her surprise and began wondering what the damned woman was doing in her bedroom, for heaven's sakes?

A question which was immediately answered by Martina. 'I hope you don't mind me invading your privacy,' she said with a wide, beaming smile. 'But I did want to have just a few quiet words with you.'

'Oh, yes…?' Lois murmured warily, going over to sit down at her dressing table, before lifting a brush and dragging it through her hair.

'Yes, well…it is a little awkward,' Martina told her,

with another brilliant, mega-watt smile. 'But the thing is…I've got quite a problem at the moment. And I thought…well, a sophisticated woman like yourself might be able to give me some good advice.'

'Advice?' Lois echoed blankly, wondering what on earth the other woman was up to now. Because she was fairly certain from what little she'd seen of her that Martina would very rarely either seek or follow the advice of *anyone*. In fact, if this clearly strong-minded and determined woman listened to anything—other than her own particular needs and ambitions—Lois would be very much surprised!

'The thing is…I'm really on the horns of a dilemma,' Martina gave a slight shrug. 'Both Ace and I are *very* worried about our daughter. Emily's a dear girl, of course. But, well, you know how it is with adolescents.'

Lois shook her head. 'No, I'm afraid I can't say that I do,' she said, keeping her back to the other woman as she continued to slowly brush her hair. 'In fact, if you're looking for advice on how to bring up teenagers, I really don't think I'm the one to give it.'

In the mirror, Lois saw Martina's lips tighten with annoyance for a moment. Clearly this interview wasn't going the way that she'd planned. And then, mastering her irritation, she gave a light, rippling laugh.

'I'm not really asking for your advice on how to bring up young girls.' She waved a delicate, dismissive hand in the air. 'No, what I'm really hoping is that you can possibly sympathise and understand my *real* problem— which is whether I ought to get back together again with my husband?'

Well! As questions go—that's a *real bummer*! Lois told herself grimly. However, she was at last beginning to see the light. Obviously this awful woman was here for a purpose—and it didn't take a particularly high IQ to work out exactly what that was.

However, Lois saw no reason why she should make life easy for Martina, so she merely gave the other woman a puzzled frown and murmured, 'I don't really see the problem...?'

'But surely you can see that it's all about female solidarity,' Martina explained. 'Surely you—as a *woman*—should be able to advise me what to do? After all, I was brought up to believe that every child needs two parents,' she added in a sanctimonious tone of voice.

'Yes, that's a good point,' Lois agreed blandly.

'Which is why I felt so really *awful* when darling Ace begged me to come back and live with him, and Emily, here at Ratcliffe Hall. And really, you know,' Martina said with a sorrowful shake of her blonde head, 'I do now see that we should *never* have got divorced. Of course, I was so young and impetuous all those years ago. And if he hadn't been so immersed in his work, and neglected his young wife, I'm sure we'd still be together today.'

'Well, if your husband thinks that you both ought to make another effort...'

'Oh, yes, he does! In fact, it was really very touching last night when he begged me—with tears in his eyes!—to take pity on a poor, lonely man. I was really...well, really quite overcome,' Martina murmured, lifting a delicate lace-edged handkerchief to her eyes.

However, Lois certainly hadn't been born yesterday! She was quite capable of seeing that there were no tears in those hard green eyes, now gazing at her with a distinctly cold, calculating look lurking within their depths.

Quite frankly, she wouldn't have believed one word of this whole rotten performance if Martina hadn't echoed Ace's own words to her, when she'd first arrived here three weeks ago. Because he had begged her, too, to take pity on 'a poor, lonely man'. It was clearly time he got hold of another script!

Putting down her hairbrush, Lois swung around on her stool. 'If you're asking me whether you should get back with your ex-husband, that must be your own decision,' she told the other woman firmly. 'Since I've never been married, I'm hardly qualified to give you any advice on such a delicate question. So, I'm afraid you're going to have to sort it out for yourselves.'

'But it's so difficult,' Martina moaned. 'I want to do the right thing by Emily, and now that Ace says that he's always, *always* loved me—and never, *ever* forgotten how happy we used to be—I really think I'm going to have to come back to him, don't you?'

Lois gave a careless shrug. There'd be plenty of time later to nurse her wounded heart. But just at the moment she was damned if she was going to give this awful woman the satisfaction of appearing to be either upset or dismayed by this bitchy, artful performance.

Because it was now quite clear to her that Martina was in her bedroom only for the purpose of issuing a strong warning. 'Keep off my turf', would be a neat précis of the information she'd quite deliberately come here to impart.

'Well, having listened to everything you've said, I really think you're probably quite right,' Lois told her, with a sage nod of her head. 'Emily clearly does need the warmth and caring protection of two parents. And if you're prepared to make the ultimate sacrifice—and *force* yourself to take pity on your ex-husband—then I think you're likely to make the right decision.

'After all,' she continued, getting into her stride and concentrating on giving one of the better performances of her life, 'I don't see how you can let the ''poor, lonely man'' languish here, all on his own. And besides...its just occurred to me,' she added, injecting a warm, enthusiastic note into her voice. 'You'd be doing yourself a real favour, too, wouldn't you?'

'I...er...I don't quite understand...'

'Well, I don't know very much about the British aristocracy, of course,' Lois told her with a careless shrug. 'But surely if you re-marry your ex-husband you'll be able to call yourself Lady Ratcliffe? A title always goes down a bomb in the States. In fact, I know quite a lot of people in Hollywood who'd just *kill* for a chance of being a real, genuine Lady!'

Although this was clearly part of her hidden agenda, Martina obviously wasn't at all pleased to have it pointed out to her quite so graphically. And neither, it seemed, was she quite so happy about Lois' enthusiastic agreement to her suggestion of getting back together with Ace.

Maybe she'd been wrong... Maybe this spectacularly beautiful redhead *wasn't* interested in her ex-husband, after all? Still, it had undoubtedly been a good idea to try and neutralise any possible threat to her plans, she told herself, as she rose slowly to her feet.

Accurately reading the thoughts clearly visible on the blonde woman's face, Lois walked across the room and opened the door.

'I'm afraid that I've got to get ready for filming,' she said with a brief smile. 'I hope I've been helpful—and good luck!' she added cheerfully, closing the door behind Martina, before breathing a heavy sigh of relief.

Half an hour later, pacing angrily up and down her bedroom, Lois still hadn't decided what to do about the situation.

Either Ace or Martina was telling a whole pack of fibs. She desperately wanted to believe that it was the sly, calculating blonde who was lying through her teeth. But it was the way they'd *both* heard Ace's description of himself as a 'poor, lonely man' which she was finding hard to swallow.

Eventually deciding that the precautions she'd already taken to keep Ace at arm's length should at least offer her some protection, Lois realised that there was at least some definite action she could take as far as the awful Martina was concerned.

Spinning around on her heel, she swiftly left the room and, after losing herself once or twice, eventually tracked down Nora Barker, Ace's old nanny and present house-keeper.

'Thank you for the sandwiches,' she began, as Nora greeted her with a beaming smile, while continuing to darn a large pair of thick woollen socks.

'I wonder if I could ask you a favour,' Lois continued, pausing for a moment as she gazed around the light, airy sitting room, which was clearly the housekeeper's domain.

'Ask away, dearie.' Nora beamed over at her.

'Well, the thing is…I'm not sure about the customs here, in England, but in America I am used to being able to lock my bedroom door. And so I wondered if it was possible for me to have a key to my room upstairs?'

Nora gave a deep rumble of laughter. 'Oh, that Master Ace! He always was a *very* naughty boy. Has he been bothering you, dearie?'

'Oh, no!' Lois protested quickly, bitterly aware of a deep flush rising up over her cheeks. 'No, it's nothing like that. Absolutely not,' she added firmly. 'In fact…you've got *quite* the wrong end of the stick.'

'Have I really, dearie? Well, well…' Nora murmured, and if Lois caught the slightly sceptical, ironic tone in her voice, she quickly decided to ignore it.

'OK—if I have to tell the truth, the fact is that I wasn't at all pleased to find Lord Ratcliffe's ex-wife in my bedroom earlier this afternoon,' Lois informed the housekeeper bluntly. 'I don't like the woman. I'm damned certain she doesn't like me. And I don't want to have to worry about her going through my things. OK?'

'Point taken, dearie.' The elderly lady nodded sagely. 'That Martina is nothing but trouble! I knew it the first moment I set eyes on the young hussy, all those years ago. And how right I was,' she added, lumbering to her feet and going over to a row of hooks on the wall. 'Here you are; this should be the right key.' She handed it to Lois. 'And don't you worry. I'll see that she doesn't bother you, again.'

'Thank you. I'm really very grateful,' Lois murmured.

'Don't be too hard on his nibs,' Nora said, as the younger woman turned and walked over to the door. 'Because I can tell that he really does think the world of you.'

'I'm simply not interested in Lord Ratcliffe,' Lois told her in a cold, crushing tone of voice as she left the room, her spirits faltering as she realised that she hadn't been able to fool Ace's old nanny. Not if that loud rumble of deeply cynical, sardonic laughter issuing from the room behind her was anything to go by!

CHAPTER SIX

As THE fifth week of the shooting schedule was drawing to a close, Lois was quite sure that she'd never felt quite so tired and exhausted.

Sitting on one of the spindly gold chairs in the large, formal drawing room, she tried to concentrate on checking over her script for the next scene.

The actual shooting of the film itself wasn't a problem. Quite remarkably, in her experience, they were well up to schedule. In fact, the director, Peter Danvers, was quietly confident of being able to bring the film in not only on time but also well within the budget.

'My first assistant is, of course, absolutely first class,' Peter had told her last night over dinner. 'We've only had one or two slip-ups. Although, it looks as if I'm going to have to re-shoot one of the bedroom scenes. Unfortunately, none of us noticed at the time that there was a heavy passenger aeroplane flying right above the house! But, all in all, I feel it's going very well.'

And, yes, it was. With only another nine days of filming to go, there was a happy and contented feeling on the set—with the camera team appearing especially cheerful. However, Lois suspected that this had more to do with the sweepstake organised amongst the crew than with anything else. Both the camera operator and the focus puller had worked with the director, Peter Danvers, many times before. As a result, they'd firmly placed their bets on him wrapping up the film by the scheduled date—and were now clearly quite confident of collecting their winnings!

So, Lois could only think that it must be her pregnancy which was causing her to feel so weary. She'd made several secret phone calls to the Harley Street doctor's consulting rooms, and had found his chief nurse very friendly and helpful. Especially over her very real worry about making love when pregnant.

'If you had a history of miscarriage, then the doctor might ask you to be careful in the first three or four months. But you sound very well and healthy, Miss Shelton,' the nurse had said soothingly. 'It can take time for a woman's body to settle down and get used to being invaded!' the girl had added with a light, sympathetic laugh. 'But it seems as if everything is coming along just fine. However, I will make an appointment for you to see the doctor just as soon as you're back in London.'

Since Lois knew that she was going to have to remain in England for two weeks after filming—to do any necessary re-recording at the London studio—that sounded the perfect time to get herself thoroughly checked out before flying home to the States.

But, of course, there was no point in fooling herself. Lois knew very well that it wasn't the filming process or her pregnancy which was causing her to feel so exhausted. She had been a busy film actress for the past ten years—it had become a way of life to wake up at five o'clock every morning, ready to arrive on the set, bright-eyed and bushy-tailed, at six o'clock precisely. And with the actual filming itself continuing for anything up to ten or eleven hours each day, she had by now trained herself and her body-clock into regarding these strange hours as a normal way of life.

No. It wasn't her professional career which was responsible. In fact, she no longer had any doubt that it was her fraught, emotionally charged private life which lay at the root of the problem. And things seemed to be going rapidly from bad to worse.

Following that extraordinary confrontation with Martina, two weeks ago, Lois really hadn't known what to make of the situation between Ace and his ex-wife.

She'd believed Ace when he'd stated that he didn't know what Martina wanted. But that was absolutely typical of a man, right? In her experience they were only too often merely pawns in the chess game of male and female relationships. Very rarely did they seem to possess either the astuteness, finesse or basic subtlety which lay within the basic genes of most women. And a good thing, too! Lois told herself with a grim smile. Goodness knows, in dealing with the masculine gender we poor females need every bit of help we can get!

But as for Martina—that was a very different story. In *her* case, the blonde woman had clearly been born with an overdose of cunning and guile. Lois had no doubt that the other woman was a nasty bit of work: totally self-absorbed and thoroughly unscrupulous. Although, for those with the wit to look beneath Martina's glossy surface, it was clear that she had as much subtlety as a herd of elephants, noisily pounding their way through the African bush.

It was quite obvious by now, to just about everyone at Ratcliffe Hall, that Martina clearly had Ace in the firing line and was determined—come hell or high water—to nail him down. Not only did she fully intend to remarry Ace and gain the title of Lady Ratcliffe—but it hadn't needed Emily's comments the other day to demonstrate how she was planning to achieve her aims.

'How's it going, kid?' Lois had asked, finding herself sitting next to the young girl at Make-Up a few days ago. 'Are you having a good time filming down in the kitchen?'

'It's all right,' Emily told her with a shrug. 'I hadn't realised that I'd have to stand around waiting for ages and ages for the cameramen and sound recordists to get everything sorted out. And then there's the make-up and costume people—they're always twitching away at my hair and clothes,' she'd added glumly. 'Quite honestly, I had no idea it was going to be so dead *boring*!'

Lois grinned. 'Well, I did warn you—didn't I?'

Emily nodded. 'You were absolutely right. In fact, I reckon it's one of the most *un*glamorous jobs I can think of. I'm seriously thinking that maybe Joe is right.'

'Oh, yes...' Lois murmured, wincing as the hairdresser accidentally stuck a pin in her head, trying to adjust some of the ribbons and feathers in her hair.

'Sorry!' the girl muttered. 'I didn't mean to...'

'That's OK,' Lois told her, before turning to Emily. 'I'm sorry, sweetie. What were you saying...?'

'Well, Joe says that being a pop star is a "right doddle". He says that while you've obviously got to have a lot of basic talent, it's just a case of turning up and recording a few songs. Do you think he's right?'

Lois shrugged. 'I can't say I know anything about the pop scene,' she muttered, leaning forward to check her make-up in the mirror. 'Who's Joe, anyway?'

'Oh, he's my sort of stepfather. Well...he's not *actually* married to my mother,' the young girl explained. 'But they've been together for ages. I like Joe,' she added with a grin. 'He's really very nice, and *terrifically* generous. And, of course,' she leaned forward to add in a confidential whisper, 'although you wouldn't think so to look at him—he's also *very* rich!'

'Oh, wow! A rich and generous stepfather can't be bad!' Lois grinned. 'Does he spoil you rotten?'

Emily laughed. 'Yes, I suppose he does. But Joe really is *very* kind—and we have lots of fun together.

Especially when he lets me go with him to the recording studios. The Raving Monsters are a great group, and—'

'Hang on!' Lois turned to look at her with startled eyes. 'You don't mean...are you telling me that your stepfather is Joe Tucker?'

'Yes! He now thinks that his stage name, "Frank N. Stein", is pretty stupid. But he and his group are so famous, that there's no point in changing it now. I think his music is absolutely wicked!'

'So do millions of other people,' Lois agreed dryly, rapidly reassessing Emily's current background—and wondering how Joe Tucker felt about Martina's protracted stay here at Ratcliffe Hall.

No wonder Ace was worried about his daughter— growing up amidst the free-spending, mega-rich world of super pop stars. Rightly or wrongly, it was an atmosphere generally regarded as totally out of touch with real life—something which Ace must be aware of, and which would clearly give him some sleepless nights.

On the other hand, it was also clear that Emily was very fond of the man who'd acted as her stepfather for a number of years. And it couldn't have been easy for the young girl to move between the two different environments of the pop scene and this large, stately home. It was a thought echoed by the youngster.

With her own hair and make-up completed, Emily waited impatiently as the girl doing Lois' hair placed a last curling ostrich feather amongst the curls at the top of her head, before checking her work and then leaving the room.

'The thing is.. ' Emily leaned closer to Lois '...I don't really know what's going to happen now. I think...well, I'm almost sure that my mother wants to come and live here, with Dad. She keeps going on and on...about how we'll all have a wonderful time. What do *you* think, Lois?'

Oh, Lord! First the mother and now the daughter asking her advice. And since she'd never been married, or had a child, how on earth was she expected to give counsel or guidance to this young and clearly troubled young girl?

'I...er...I really don't know what to say,' Lois murmured. 'I know it's difficult at your age, coping with grown-ups. And although I know you love your father...'

'Oh, yes—I do!'

'But you also love your mother, as well?'

'Yes, but...'

'So, I expect you sometimes feel like the Push-me-pull-you animal in the Dr Doolittle stories. I used to feel the same,' Lois added, with a sympathetic smile. 'My parents broke up when I was just a little bit older than you. And it was all very confusing. All I wanted to do was to please them both. But, of course, they wanted different things. So it was very difficult. Is that how you're feeling at the moment?'

Emily nodded her head vigorously. 'Yes, that's *exactly* how I feel. In fact,' she added slowly, 'I just wish that we could all go back to how it used to be, a month ago. I mean...everything seems to be changing. I love my dad, but I was quite happy living with Joe and my mother, and having fun with all my friends at school.

'But now Mummy says that she and my dad might be getting married again,' the girl continued in an agitated voice. 'She says that he's really, *really* miserable about not seeing me every day. And...and it will be all *my* fault if he grows into an unhappy old man. Which means that I'll have to come and live down here all the time. I won't see any of my old schoolfriends. Besides...what's

going to happen to Joe?' she added plaintively, before
suddenly bursting into tears.

'It's all right, sweetie,' Lois murmured, putting her
arms about the thin, scrawny figure of the young girl.
'I'm sure everything will work out for the best.'

However, looking back at that sad scene now, as she
sat on a spindly Hepplewhite chair in the blue and gold
drawing room while the film technicians arranged the
next shot, Lois couldn't help thinking that it sounded
highly unlikely that everything would work out for the
best.

She'd felt so desperately sorry for the poor kid. It was
totally immoral and truly evil of Martina to put such
extreme, heavy pressure on a young girl—merely for her
own diabolically selfish ends. Because while Ace clearly
loved his daughter, and would, Lois suspected, do just
about anything he could for Emily, he would *never*
countenance messing around with a teenager's mind and
emotions, as her mother appeared to be doing.

In fact, listening to Emily, she'd found herself transported back to the miserably unhappy time when her
own parents had split up. And, of course, amidst all the
drama and tension *all* she'd ever wanted—and had desperately prayed for—had been to return to her previously
safe, secure life. However, the circumstances weren't exactly the same as far as Emily was concerned.

However devious Martina might be, she'd been quite
right when she'd stated that every child needed two parents. But, since the young girl had obviously lived in
happiness and contentment with her mother and Joe
Tucker, it wasn't easy to see whether it would really be
in Emily's best interests to live with her original mother
and father.

And what about Ace? What did he really think about
the situation? Being obviously so fond of his young

daughter, he might well feel that he had both a duty and an obligation to try and make another go of life with Martina. Over the weeks she'd been here at Ratcliffe Hall, Lois had come to see that he was a very sincere and thoughtful man, who took his responsibilities very seriously.

He was also a deeply honourable man. Because, while he obviously didn't like it, he'd accepted at face value her explanation of exactly why it was *so* important—if only for the sake of her future career—for him to keep totally silent about their previous meeting in the Philippines.

But, while he might have agreed to put up with the situation, he'd insisted on keeping Lois to her promise. In fact, Ace clearly regarded it as the perfect solution to their problems. But she wasn't at all sure. Because while the basic *idea* of joining him in his suite of rooms for coffee in the evening hadn't sounded too unreasonable, she was finding it increasingly difficult to cope with in practice.

Initially, of course, she hadn't been at all keen on the arrangement. One of the reasons for her reluctance being that she had no idea about Martina's accommodation in this large house. She certainly didn't want to have to have anything to do with the awful woman—who would definitely *not* be at all pleased to find Lois in her ex-husband's apartments.

However, Ace had made it quite clear on the first evening she'd joined him after dinner that he was only letting Martina continue to stay on at Ratcliffe Hall because she was Emily's mother.

'I've told the damned irritating woman that if she puts one foot on my side of the house I'll send her straight back to London!' he'd added with a grim laugh, before saying that he'd had quite enough of his ex-wife for one day—and could they *please* change the subject!

Sitting curled up on one of the large sofas in Ace's equally large sitting room, they'd talked for hours and hours over the past two weeks, exchanging details and stories of their past lives and discovering each other's likes and dislikes.

Indeed, as far as cementing and deepening a relationship was concerned, it was undoubtedly the perfect arrangement. But Ace, that honourable man, had rigidly kept to his promise not to touch her until she'd finished filming. And, while she did certainly appreciate a guy who could keep his word, Lois was finding it a definite strain on her emotions.

She knew it was perverse of her. She knew that after having exacted a promise from him she was being deeply unreasonable. But she found herself desperately wishing that he would occasionally break out of his mental straitjacket…roughly sweeping her up into his arms and obliterating all her doubts and fears in a searing outburst of burning passion.

In fact, Ace *had* broken down once—which had made his subsequent iron-like control of his emotions so difficult to cope with.

It had been an evening when they'd been talking later than usual. Just as she was about to leave the room, he'd quickly caught hold of her arm, fiercely pulling her to him as his mouth possessed hers in a hard, determined fashion, silencing any protest she might have made.

But protest had been just about the very *last* thing on her mind. Lois had known, without a shadow of a doubt, that she wanted him more than she'd wanted anything in her whole life. And to hell with the consequences!

Her senses had seemed drugged by the evocative, musky scent of his cologne. A raging excitement had seized her as his strong hands roughly caressed her body, and she'd trembled helplessly in the clutches of an overwhelming passionate longing for fulfilment that demanded satisfaction, responding blindly to the savage forces of need and desire, and the evidence, in the hard-muscled thighs pressed so closely to hers, of his own arousal.

But it had been an all too brief embrace. Even while drowning in a pool of dark passion, shivering as his mouth had trailed slowly down the long column of her neck, she'd heard him swearing grimly under his breath. And, before she knew what was happening, Lois had found herself being pushed roughly out into the dark corridor, the door to his sitting room being slammed shut with a resounding thud.

Fortuitously, it seemed, Ace had been forced to go away on business, attending an agricultural seminar for a few days following that briefly passionate encounter. And it was definitely lucky that he hadn't been around when Neil Gray, to her total dismay and confusion, had suddenly lost his marbles!

They'd just finished filming a scene in the library, which had involved Lois—in her role of a beautiful but thoroughly wicked, designing woman—flirting heavily with Neil, before pretending to trip over a rug, allowing him to catch her in his arms.

It had seemed to involve goodness knows how many takes, there being first a problem with the camera, and then the director deciding that he wanted changes in the lighting. And she had, admittedly, seemed to have spent a large part of the evening in Neil's arms. Even so, there had been absolutely no excuse for what had happened next!

By the time they'd finished filming, late in the evening, Lois was feeling thoroughly worn out. Which was probably why she'd been so slow to react when Neil had caught hold of her arm as she was making her way back to her dressing room, pulling her into a small side room—and proceeding to declare his undying love!

'Oh, come on!' she'd protested with a slight laugh, half thinking that this must be some kind of joke on his part. 'It's been one hell of a day, and I really am tired. So, why don't we—?'

'You don't understand,' he muttered huskily, clasping his arms about her and showering her face with kisses.

'*Please*! This is absolutely ridiculous!' she gasped, desperately trying to wriggle free from his embrace.

But Neil clearly wasn't getting the message. 'I'm crazy about you,' he muttered, trying to get a firm grip of the woman twisting and turning in his arms.

'Stop this—*at once*!' she cried, at last breaking free and glowering up at him as she readjusted her costume, which had slipped off one shoulder. 'What on earth's got into you?'

'I'm crazy about you,' he repeated hoarsely.

'Well—I can certainly see that you're temporarily out of your mind!' she retorted grimly.

'Come on, baby!' he pleaded. 'I just know that we could make beautiful music together.'

To hear such a hackneyed phrase pronounced in an upper-crust English accent proved too much for Lois. Her anger draining rapidly away, she couldn't help but see the amusing side of the situation.

'Relax, kid—and do yourself a favour!' She grinned. 'I won't say that I'm not flattered, because of course I am. But, hey—I guess I must be at least a few years older than you, right?'

'I don't care about that,' Neil muttered glumly, a deep flush rising over his swarthy features as she gave a chuckle of laughter.

'Look here,' she said, giving his arm a friendly pat, 'I'm thirty-two years of age. And, while it's not exactly long in the tooth, it does mean that by now I've learned not to fool around with my leading men. Especially not with smart young guys five or six years younger than myself.'

'I'm nearly twenty-eight,' he protested sulkily.

'Wow! That sounds *really* ancient!' she teased, before realising that it was no good just giving this guy a sharp set-down. There were still some days of filming to go. And neither of them could afford to let a 'situation' develop, which could affect their performances.

'The fact is, kid, I think you're going to be a really great, successful actor,' she told him seriously. 'I'm thoroughly enjoying doing this film with you, and if we get *really* lucky it could be a smash hit.

'What's more,' she went on as he continued to stare down at her in sullen silence, 'I reckon that you could turn out to be England's latest sex symbol.'

'Do you really think so?' he muttered, clearly beginning to cheer up.

'Yes, I do. So, you'd better start getting fit!' she grinned. 'Because I reckon you're going to get pretty exhausted—fighting off all those gorgeous young girls, who'll be *dying* to date the latest heart-throb!'

By now Neil was definitely looking brighter, and clearly feeling a whole lot better about himself. Besides, she had, in fact, said no more than the truth. He *was* a highly attractive young man. And, once the film-going public had a good look at him in those tight pantaloons, he was likely to find himself in great demand!

'You're not kidding me?'

'Absolutely not!' Lois assured him earnestly, being very careful not to show, by even the flicker of an eye-lash, that she was secretly amused to discover that

Neil—along with so many of his fellow actors—could take any amount of flattery. Especially if it was laid on with a heavy trowel.

'So…how about if we forget this whole incident?' she murmured, before turning towards the door. 'And in any case, you really ought to take pity on poor Phoebe.'

'Phoebe?'

Lois turned around as she opened the door. 'Yes. You know…that young girl who collapsed with nerves the first day we were filming? You were so sweet and kind to her, remember? Well, all I can say,' Lois continued as he nodded his head, 'is that she's clearly been carrying a torch for you over the last few weeks. I reckon you ought to do something about it, don't you?' she added, before slipping silently out of the room.

Grinning with satisfaction at having given young Neil something to think about—and, hopefully, managed to keep their working relationship on an even keel—Lois had hurried off to her dressing room.

And she'd been quite right. After a few awkward moments the next day, Neil and she had settled down to their normal working pattern. And, most fortuitously of all, he and Phoebe now seemed to be an item.

However, while she seemed to have sorted out one possible problem, her life still seemed to contain enough complications to make her dizzy. And it was her very real, actual bouts of dizziness which were particularly worrying her at the moment.

There has been two occasions, yesterday, when, right in the middle of a scene, she'd suddenly had an extraordinarily peculiar sensation that the world was spinning around her and that she would fall to the floor any minute. She had, of course, quickly pulled herself together. But it had been not only disturbing, but also a little frightening at the time. In fact…

Her thoughts were interrupted as the assistant director
announced that they were ready to begin filming.

'OK, everyone on set, please,' he called out, waving
to the make-up girl and Peggy Fraser to have a last-
minute check of Lois' make-up and costume.

'You're looking a little pale today,' the make-up girl
muttered, quickly painting some more blusher on Lois'
cheeks. And Peggy, too, frowned as she made some ad-
justments to the actress's low-cut, heavy gold satin costume.

'Are you sure you're getting enough to eat?' she muttered, quickly tightening the band beneath Lois' bosom.
'Because this last week you seem to have lost weight
rather than put it on.'

Lois smiled. 'Surely that can only be a good thing?'
she murmured, before going over to stand beside the
large marble fireplace.

Everything seemed to be going wrong today, she
thought wearily as the director called for yet another
take. They seemed to have been doing this scene for
hours! Quite apart from anything else, her ankles felt
swollen and uncomfortable, the gold-buckled shoes beginning to pinch her tired feet. Standing here for so long
was nothing but a real drag.

And then, as the director was calling for what he
promised would be the last take, she found herself assailed by another attack of dizziness; everything spun
about her glazed eyes, and there was nothing she could
do to prevent herself as she clutched in vain at the
mantelpiece, before falling down onto the floor.

'I'm sorry...I'm so sorry...' she muttered helplessly
some moments later, as she found herself being helped
up to her feet. 'I...I'm sure I'm going to be all right,'
she gasped, swaying dangerously as the director called

out to one of the larger technicians, asking him to carry
Miss Shelton upstairs to her bedroom.

'I want you to go and rest,' Peter Danvers told her
firmly. 'Take the rest of the day off—and don't worry
about anything. We're slightly ahead of schedule, so
there's no need to worry,' he added, giving her a rather
awkward pat on the shoulder, before going off to confer
with his cameramen.

'I don't know what's wrong with me...' Lois muttered
tearfully as Peggy helped her off with her costume upstairs in the bedroom. 'I feel such a...such an idiot!' she
muttered, seemingly unable to prevent helpless tears
from trickling down her cheeks.

'Relax. I expect you're just tired,' Peggy muttered
soothingly. 'It's been a long, hard five weeks, and you'll
feel much better after a good long sleep.'

But there seemed nothing she could do to help the
girl, who was by now weeping in earnest. Peggy gazed
down at her with a worried frown, biting her lips and
wondering what on earth she ought to do next, when
help arrived in the form of Lord Ratcliffe's housekeeper.

'Well, here's a to-do!' the elderly woman said as she
knocked, then entered the room, before turning to Peggy.
'How is the poor dear?'

Peggy shrugged helplessly. 'I honestly don't know,'
she said, turning to look at the hunched, huddled figure
of Lois, whose slim shoulders shook as she sobbed into
the pillow.

'I'm sure there's no need to worry,' Nora told her.
'First-time babies can be a very emotional experience,
you know.'

Peggy's startled eyes flew to her face. 'How did you
know...? I mean, I don't think I quite...'

'How did I know that she's pregnant?' Nora chuckled.
'If you'd seen as many mothers and babies as I have,

dearie, you wouldn't have any problem in guessing the condition she's in. Why, I knew it the moment I set eyes on the poor lamb.

'Now, you just stop that crying, Miss Lois,' she added, going over to the bed and leaning over to put a comforting arm around the girl's shoulder. 'It's time to dry those tears. Old Nora will soon have you feeling nice and comfortable again.'

'I feel such an idiot!' Lois muttered, blowing her nose as she sat up in the bed, some moments later. 'I really thought I could cope. I truly believed, since it was so early on in my pregnancy, that there wouldn't be any problems.'

'All mothers are different—just like their babies,' Nora told her firmly. 'And while some women sail through their pregnancies without any problems, it can take others a few months to settle down. But there's no need to worry. We'll have you feeling better in no time,' she promised, before turning to Peggy. 'We just have to make sure that she has enough rest, and puts her feet up whenever possible. And eats properly too, of course.'

'I just can't seem to face any food at the moment,' Lois moaned, brushing a hand through her curly hair. 'Just looking at the stuff on the plate makes me feel nauseous.'

'Good wholesome food and regular exercise is what you need,' Nora stated confidently. 'And I'll make sure that you get it,' she added with another of her rumbling laughs.

However, although Lois might still be feeling upset, she was perfectly capable of noting that the old nanny had made no mention of, nor raised any questions about the father of her baby. And, while she'd allowed Peggy to assume that it was one of her old boyfriends, Nora's

ominous silence on the subject showed that she clearly
had a very good idea of exactly *who* was responsible.

'When is the baby due, dearie?'

Lois shrugged. 'Oh, I'm not quite sure. Around
Christmas time, I think. Although—'

Her words were interrupted by a loud gasp from
across the room. Peggy and Nora turned around to see
Emily standing in the doorway.

'Hi, kid...' Lois muttered feebly as the girl, giving
the occupants of the room another quick, startled glance,
swiftly turned on her heels and disappeared from sight.

'*Oh, Lord*! That's torn it!' Lois groaned, throwing herself back on the pillows. 'She must have heard every
word we were saying.'

Nora shrugged. 'I'm sure there's no need to worry,
dearie. Little Miss Emily will be thrilled to think that
you're having a baby.'

'I'm not concerned about whether she likes the idea
or not. That's *not* the problem!' Lois cried tearfully. 'Far
more to the point is that if we don't do something the
news of my pregnancy is going to be all over the film
set...in five seconds flat.'

'She's right,' Peggy told Nora with a worried frown.
'Emily is a dear girl—but silent she isn't!'

'We've got to stop her!' Lois said quickly, throwing
back the sheet and scrambling to her feet, to stand swaying beside the bed. 'Because if she tells anyone—and I
mean *anyone*—we're all in deep, *deep* trouble!'

CHAPTER SEVEN

HURRIEDLY pulling on a pair of lightweight navy blue linen trousers and a matching short-sleeved cotton shirt, Lois dashed past the astonished gaze of both Nora and Peggy Fraser, out through the door and on down the corridor.

Pray heaven she wasn't too late! Lois told herself breathlessly, hoping against hope that—as she herself would have done at the same age—Emily had taken refuge in her own bedroom.

Arriving panting outside the door, she knocked and peered inside the bedroom. Yes, she'd been quite right. Because there, curled up in a ball on the small, single four-poster bed, was the thin, scrawny figure of Ace's daughter.

Despite knowing that she was guilty of being slightly callous, Lois still couldn't help breathing a deep sigh of relief as she moved slowly across the room. However, not quite knowing what to say under such circumstances, she sat down on the mattress beside the young girl, before quietly placing a soft, gentle hand on Emily's shoulder.

There was a long silence for some moments. But when Emily didn't shrug off the gentle pressure of her fingers, merely remained huddled up in a foetal position, Lois took a deep breath.

'Emily…?' she murmured, pausing as she wondered what on earth she could say.

But the decision was taken from her hands as Emily

quickly rolled back to face her, roughly brushing a hand across her damp eyelids.

'I'm so sorry, Lois. I really didn't mean…I don't want you to think that I go around snooping on other people's conversations,' she muttered tearfully, avoiding Lois' eyes as she stared fixedly down at her thin fingers, nervously picking at the raised design of her bed cover.

'I never thought that. It's just—'

'I'm really *not* an eavesdropper!' Emily told her. 'In fact, I really, *really* hate people who hang around trying to listen into my own private conversations, and…'

'Darling—*please*!' Lois quickly put her arms around the girl's thin shoulders in a warm, comfortable hug. 'It would *never* have occurred to me that you'd deliberately been listening to a private conversation. Absolutely *never*!' she repeated firmly. 'I'm merely here because I didn't want you to be upset in any way by what you've just accidentally overheard.'

The girl raised her tear-stained face, staring at Lois in surprise. 'What…? Do you mean that bit about you expecting a baby?'

'Yes. I…I just thought you might be rather shocked, and…'

'But why should I be worried about it?' Emily asked with a puzzled frown.

'Well…' Lois paused, relieved to note that the teenager didn't seem unduly upset by the thought of her pregnancy. But she wasn't at all sure how to proceed from here. 'The thing is, kid, I'm not married. And there are many people who would think, probably quite rightly, that I ought to have a husband before giving birth to a child.'

'Oh, nobody minds about that sort of thing nowadays,' Emily told her with a shrug. 'Lots of Joe's friends in the pop world don't believe in getting married, even though some of them have got children.'

Feeling rather shocked at the fourteen-year-old's seemingly sophisticated almost blasé approach to marriage and motherhood, Lois felt constrained to point out that the way of life enjoyed by some of the mega-rich pop stars was definitely *not* ideal—as far as normal family life was concerned.

'Unfortunately, as I know from talking to one or two of my friends, it's a tough life being a single parent— even if you've got oodles of money,' she told the girl firmly. 'And for those who haven't, and find themselves living on the breadline—it's a desperately hard, lonely struggle trying to bring up a child on your own. In fact, as your mother said the other day, "Every child needs two parents". And she was quite right,' Lois added forcefully, anxious to make sure that the young girl got the message.

'However, I didn't come here to give you a lecture,' Lois continued with a slightly rueful smile. 'I just wanted to make sure that you didn't make the same stupid mistake as I have, right?'

Emily nodded. 'I do understand what you're saying. But...' She hesitated for a moment, and then went on, 'Are you going to marry the father of your baby?'

'No, I'm afraid this story doesn't have a happy ending, Emily. But that's my problem, right?' she said, quickly deciding to turn the conversation onto quite a different tack.

'Although I know that you are still very young, I feel you're perfectly capable of understanding what I'm now going to say,' Lois stated firmly, before explaining the likely difficulties and problems which would arise if the American backers of the film learned about her pregnancy.

'So, I'm sure you can see why it's so *desperately* important that you tell no one about the fact that I'm expecting a baby. It isn't just my career which is on the line,' Lois added with a rueful shrug of her shoulders. 'It would affect everyone concerned with this production. And, after all—' she gave a slight laugh '—I'd hate to think that *you* might lose your moment of stardom!'

Emily grinned. 'Actually, I've now definitely decided that I *don't* want to be a film star. And I've rather gone off the whole idea of being something big in the pop world, too. In fact...' she glanced shyly up at Lois '...I rather think...well, in the last few days I've decided that what I *really* would like to do would be to learn to be a film director.'

'Oh, really?' Lois murmured, trying not to smile as she remembered herself at Emily's age, changing her mind practically every week as she picked and discarded the ideas of different professions.

'I think it's a really cool job. And being a director means that you're in charge of absolutely everything, doesn't it? I've been watching how Mr Danvers makes everyone do what *he* wants,' she added enthusiastically. 'I mean...he's obviously got a sort of idea, in his head, of how he wants to tell the story. And I think that's really interesting.'

Well! Lois thought with surprise. It was clear that the young girl had certainly been doing her homework. And she'd quickly assimilated the importance of a director's role in film-making. Maybe it might be the profession for her, after all. However, that would all lie very much in the future. The important thing at present was to ensure Emily's total silence.

'I know that I can rely on you to keep silent as the grave about this baby of mine,' Lois said, rising slowly to her feet. 'And when I asked you not to tell anyone—

do please remember that that includes your father and mother, right?'

Emily nodded as Lois walked towards the door. 'I promise not to tell anyone—anyone at all.'

It was going to be yet another hot sunny day, Lois thought, walking slowly through the fragrant rose garden lying beside Ace's wing of the large, stately house.

The dew was still thick on the ground as she crossed a wide green lawn before, shivering slightly in the fresh morning air, she decided to make her way towards a large clump of trees on the other side of the park.

On reaching the woodland glade, she sank down onto a small wooden bench, leaning back to absorb the magnificent view of rolling countryside laid out before her.

It was, quite frankly, a considerable relief to have left behind the house, her work on the film—and all the worry about Emily's discovery of her pregnancy two days ago. Although, to be fair, she was feeling a lot better in herself. As Nora had forecast, feeling dizzy and lapsing into such a stupid faint had undoubtedly been due to overwork and lack of food. And now that Ace's old nanny was making her eat sensibly—standing grimly over her while she consumed a large English breakfast in the privacy of her bedroom—there was no doubt that she was feeling a whole lot better.

Not that she'd seen very much of Nora over the past two days. Other than the older woman's bustling arrival, early every morning, the housekeeper seemed totally absorbed with organising a surprise party for Ace's fortieth birthday. It apparently had to be a deep secret.

'If his nibs got wind of what I'm up to he'd have a blue fit!' Nora had told her with a chuckle, explaining how she was not only inviting his immediate family but all the film crew as well, from the director right down to the lowliest make-up assistant.

'It's going to be a right good do! So, not a word to anyone, mind?' she'd added, before bustling off with the breakfast tray to concentrate on icing the huge cake which she'd made some days ago.

And that made *two* secrets floating around the huge house, Lois grimly reminded herself. While knowing that she could, of course, count on the silence of both Nora and Peggy, she'd been very nervous of having to ask Emily to keep her lips firmly buttoned up. But, other than a cheeky wink every now and then, the young girl seemed to have kept her word.

So far so good. Luckily, with only seven days to go before the end of filming, there was a good chance that she could get out of this mess totally unscathed. And, since there was so much of the film already in the can, it was likely that if and when the news *did* leak out about her expecting a baby—which it was almost certain to do, since she certainly wasn't getting any thinner!—it wouldn't make any financial sense for Sol Weiser to kill off the production.

So, it looked as if her only real major problem was Ace himself. But, since she'd be leaving here in a week's time, and would soon be back in America, there was no reason why he should ever find out about her pregnancy. Particularly since he knew nothing about show business and hardly ever went to the cinema—two statements which she recalled him making at their first meeting— and was therefore extremely unlikely to read or hear any gossip about the film world.

So, why wasn't she feeling happier about the situation? Everything was working out just fine, right? So, why was she sitting here feeling so depressed, and stupidly wishing that everything could be so very different?

With a deep, unhappy sigh she leaned back on the bench, shutting her eyes against the early-morning sun. There were times when she reckoned 'life' was definitely a four-letter word!

Here she was, aching and trembling for a guy who wasn't just the father of her forthcoming child but with whom she now realised she was deeply in love. *And she couldn't do a damn thing about it!* Not when there was a good chance that he could be pressured into getting back together with Martina.

Ace obviously took his role as a father very seriously. And if his ex-wife managed to convince him that it was in Emily's best interests for them to resume their married life—he would have to be ultra-stony-hearted and uncaring about his young daughter's welfare not to give it *very* serious consideration. And, because she loved him, Lois knew that she could do nothing but stand silently by while he made his decision.

Come on—pull yourself together, she told herself roughly. Sitting here and mooning over Ace wasn't going to achieve anything, was it? Time was supposed to be a great healer. So, she'd just have to grit her teeth and concentrate on being the best possible mother for their child.

Knowing that she was going to be severely cross-questioned by Nora about whether she'd taken a proper amount of exercise this morning, Lois rose to her feet. She wasn't needed on set until this afternoon, and therefore it seemed a good idea to explore the perimeter of the park.

However, she hadn't gone very far when the peace and quiet was disturbed by the sound of an engine. Turning around, she saw a large car careering over the grass towards her.

'Hop in,' Ace called out, leaning across to open the passenger door of a large Range Rover.

'No…well, I mean, I was just going for a walk around the park,' she said hesitantly, feeling an idiot to find herself flushing beneath the gleam in his heavily lidded eyes as they swept over her nervous figure.

'You can do that any time,' he told her brusquely. 'I've got to make a quick trip into Lewes. It's the county town of East Sussex, and I thought you might be interested to see a typically old English town, plus the remains of an old castle. And before you bother to try and think of a good excuse not to join me,' he added with a grim laugh, impatiently beating his fingers on the steering wheel, 'I've already checked the film schedule, and I know that you aren't needed until this afternoon.'

Hesitating, and well aware of the voice at the back of her head telling her that this was a very, *very* bad idea, Lois couldn't seem to decide what to do. On one hand…

'For God's sake, woman! Stop dithering and get in the car,' Ace barked irritably.

'Oh, all right.' She shrugged. He clearly wasn't going to take no for an answer. And she couldn't deny that it would be a welcome change to escape, for a short time at least, from the hustle and bustle of Ratcliffe Hall.

Sitting beside Ace in the Range Rover, which he clearly used for travelling about his large estate, she glanced sideways through her eyelashes at his hawk-like profile. Beneath its tan, his face looked pale and strained. Oh, dear, maybe the few days he'd spent on a course concerning management of estates hadn't been a success, she thought, suddenly feeling guilty of having been so immersed in her own problems that she'd given very little thought to any he might have regarding his new inheritance.

*　　*　　*

Lewes certainly looked an interesting place, and Lois found herself excited at the idea of exploring the town while Ace visited a local farm machinery dealer, agreeing to meet up with him in an hour's time at the White Hart Hotel.

Having purchased a local guidebook, she wandered around the streets, wishing she had enough time to explore the castle, whose foundations apparently dated from the time of William the Conqueror. However, she did manage to find Anne of Cleves' house, without getting lost too many times, and was delighted to view the many elegant Georgian houses in the high street. Unfortunately, she barely had time to read about Thomas Paine, who'd been a customs man in the town before writing *The Rights of Man*, before having to join Ace and return to Ratcliffe Hall.

'Thanks for the trip into town,' she murmured, leaning back in her seat. In fact, Lois was just thinking what a pleasant morning it had been when it gradually began to occur to her that they didn't seem to be returning by the same route they'd taken when driving to the town.

'Are you going back a different way?' she muttered, frowning as she peered out of the window of the Range Rover. 'This doesn't look at all like the same road...'

'You're quite right—it isn't. I've decided that we're going to have an early lunch at a small country restaurant which I discovered soon after coming down to live here.'

'But...I can't possibly...I have to get back...'

'I'm quite aware of your schedule. Which is precisely why I booked an early table,' he told her blandly, not taking a blind bit of notice of her protests as the Range Rover sped through the country lanes. 'I'll have you back at Ratcliffe Hall in plenty of time for your afternoon filming session, right?'

'Of course, it's not ''right'',' she snapped. 'If there's

one thing I *really* hate, it's guys doing their macho bit—
and ordering me around.'

'Well, it's up to you,' he drawled, and her irritation
increased as she noticed his lips twitching with laughter
as he brought the vehicle to a halt outside a pretty, half-
timbered building. 'I'm going to have lunch anyway. So,
if you want to stay here in the Range Rover for the next
hour—that's entirely up to you,' he added, switching off
the engine and turning to her with an amused smile on
his face.

'Don't you patronise me, you...you foul man!' she
retorted angrily, swearing under her breath as she wres-
tled with the catch on her seat belt. 'You go and have
your lunch. Just leave the keys in the ignition and I'll
drive myself back to Ratcliffe Hall, thank you very
much!'

'What on earth's wrong with you?' he demanded, the
amusement dying on his face.

'There's *nothing* wrong with me,' she shouted furiously, aware with one part of her mind that she was
behaving badly, but somehow quite unable to combat
the almost overpowering urge to hit out at the man sitting beside her. And why she was feeling this way, she
had absolutely no idea.

'I've had quite enough of this nonsense!' he grated
angrily, swiftly releasing both their seat belts, before
gripping hold of her shoulders and pulling her towards
him. Holding her imprisoned against his hard figure, he
waited for a few moments, but when she continued to
struggle and protest strongly against his treatment he
simply lowered his dark head, firmly possessing her
mouth with his own and effectively silencing all further
protests.

His lips were hard and unyielding, but even as she
took a deep breath and opened her mouth to cry out she

only succeeded in making his kiss even more intimate. Gradually, a soft weakness invaded her body, replacing the sharp surge of aggression, and she found herself meekly surrendering to the dynamically masculine strength of his embrace.

And, then of course, she knew. She knew that this was what she had wanted so badly: to be once again clasped tightly in his arms, and to have his lips pressed so firmly to her own.

'Well…?' Ace murmured, raising his dark head and gazing down into her dazed eyes. 'Do you think we could now go inside the restaurant and have a quiet lunch?' he drawled wryly. 'I hate having any arguments with you, Lois. And God knows what got into you just now. But I'm damned if I'm going to put up with any more of that sort of nonsense. Got the message?' he demanded, as she struggled to pull herself together.

'Yes… I…'

'I've already said that I'll get you back to the Hall in plenty of time for the afternoon film session,' he said firmly, before his harsh expression gave way to an infectious grin. 'Quite frankly, darling, you might take pity on me. I somehow missed breakfast this morning—and I'm absolutely starving!'

'Oh, well…in that case it doesn't sound as if I've got any choice, does it?' she muttered, as he came around to help her down from the vehicle.

'Not a lot!' he agreed cheerfully, taking no notice of the quick scowl she threw in his direction as he propelled her firmly in front of him into the restaurant.

'There—that wasn't so bad, was it?' He grinned as they sat sipping their coffee at the end of the meal. 'Come on, Lois—why don't you confess that it *was* a good idea to have a break from filming?'

She gave him a sheepish grin. 'Yes, you're quite right,' she admitted. Because it had been a really delicious meal. And, as always, she'd found herself responding to the warm, relaxed charm of the man sitting opposite her. But she was also perfectly well aware that she was playing with fire. Her first, instinctive feeling that she should not get into his Range Rover had been quite correct.

Meetings such as this—and especially that brief but intense embrace in the vehicle outside this restaurant—merely reinforced the deep feelings she had for Ace. And, since they had no future together, she must...she really *must* force herself to stay well away from this highly disturbing and also highly dangerous man.

'I...I really do think that we ought to be getting back now,' she murmured, glancing down at her wristwatch.

'Anything you say. As always—I'm entirely at your command,' he drawled mockingly as he rose to go over and pay the bill.

'That'll be the day!' she muttered under her breath. But she was fairly certain, from his deep rumble of laughter, that he had heard exactly what she'd said.

The next two days passed fairly peacefully. Determined to keep to his schedule, the director was working everyone very hard. And, since Lois appeared to be in virtually every scene of the film, she was too tired to do anything other than fall exhausted into bed after dinner each evening. Only a disturbing encounter this evening, with Martina, had seemed to disturb the even tenor of her existence.

After finishing her meal, and leaving the film crew all happily enjoying their coffee and the occasional glass of whisky down in the kitchen, Lois had been slowly mounting the main staircase when she'd met Martina coming down towards her.

'Have you missed supper?' Lois had murmured idly, not recalling having seen the other woman at dinner tonight. But then, there were so many tables in the huge old kitchen that it was maybe not surprising she had missed her amongst the crowd of actors and film crew.

'No, I've had better things to do,' Martina announced imperiously, pausing to rake Lois' tired figure with a distinctly unfriendly gleam in her sharp, cat-like green eyes.

Lois was just thinking that this blonde woman was becoming more arrogant with each succeeding day—clearly practising for her new role as Lady of the Manor—when Martina placed a hand firmly on her arm.

'I've had a funny feeling, ever since I came here that there was definitely something going on between you and Ace,' she hissed, her voice sounding both venomous and oddly triumphant as it echoed around the silent staircase.

'Don't be ridiculous,' Lois muttered, trying to pull her arm away from the fierce, claw-like grip of the other woman. 'And in any case—what has it got to do with you? Surely Lord Ratcliffe is your *ex*-husband?' she added, before feeling ashamed of allowing herself to get involved in trading insults with this poisonous woman.

Martina gave a high-pitched trill of laughter. 'Don't worry,' she sneered. 'I won't have any problem getting back together with Ace! Not now. Not when I know exactly how to cook *your* goose!' she added, with another shrill, triumphant laugh, before running on down the stairs towards the hall.

Baffled by the weird, strange undercurrents which seemed to have lain behind the brief encounter, and feeling, as always, highly uncomfortable after an encounter with the blonde woman, Lois had merely shrugged her shoulders before continuing on up the stairs towards her room.

As far as Ace and his ex-wife were concerned she had a completely clear conscience. He had given her his word that he hadn't been involved with anyone else when they'd first met on that Philippine island. And even since arriving here, at Ratcliffe Hall, he'd constantly assured her that he had absolutely no intention of having anything to do with his ex-wife.

Despite everything he'd said, Lois knew that not only did Martina have Ace very firmly in her sights, but also intended—by hook or by crook—to become the new chatelaine of Ratcliffe Hall. However, it was the question of Emily's welfare which presented the biggest problem, causing Lois to be super-cautious as far as her relationship with Ace was concerned.

She'd always known that Ace would probably, when push came to shove, feel that his responsibilities towards Emily must come before any other consideration. And it was this duty and care for his daughter which would be likely to propel him towards a reconciliation with his ex-wife. Which was precisely why, despite being deeply in love with the man, Lois always tried to guard her own emotional response to Ace.

The last time she'd fallen so heavily in love it had proved to be an utterly humiliating experience. And there were so *many* parallels between that romance and her current situation. Then, too, she'd come to care deeply for a tall, dark and handsome Englishman. And he, too, it had appeared later, had a beautiful ex-wife in the background.

However, while Ross Whitney had never been actually divorced from his wife—although they'd been separated for a long time—Lois had found herself caught up in a complicated marital situation. And what had happened? An *exact* copy of what was going on now, at Ratcliffe Hall—that was what had happened! Because, Ross' wife had turned up, and before you could say abracadabra...they'd gone off holding hands into the sunset together.

Well! She might have been a fool once, but she sure as hell wasn't going to be taken for a patsy twice running!

So, finding herself once again in the same sort of situation, it wasn't surprising that she was being as cautious as all-get-out, Lois told herself grimly as she climbed wearily into bed. She would be a damn fool to be anything else.

'How can you torment me so, Reginald?' Lois cried, coquettishly peering over the top of her fan at Neil Gray in his role as Reginald de Courcy as they stood facing each other beside the large marble mantelpiece in the hall. 'How can you say that you're devoted to me, heart and soul—and yet care for another?'

This scene was going really rather well, she thought, thankful that various 'bugs' had been overcome during the early part of this morning's filming. However, as Neil dropped to one knee, pledging his undying love for the glamorous Lady Susan, they were suddenly startled by the sound of a large 'thud' and screams of rage, followed by a loud banging of doors in the distance.

'*Cut!*' the director growled, as the noise seemed to grow louder, accompanied by the noise of various bangs and pounding of feet—and what sounded remarkably like a violent explosion of breaking glass, as though someone was throwing heavy objects through the upstairs windows.

'What on earth is going on?' Neil muttered, rising to

his feet. 'It sounds like World War III is breaking out around here.'

Lois shrugged, as confused as the rest of the film crew, who'd all stopped doing their various jobs as they, and the other actors, listened goggle-eyed to the ever-increasing commotion.

As the sounds of rage and fury mounted, they were stunned by the sight of Martina, looking distraught as she ran into the hall.

Startled, she gazed about her for a moment before screaming, 'And you can all go to hell, as well!' then rushing blindly across the marble floor, knocking over a floodlight and brushing one of the sound recordists roughly out of her way before she disappeared from sight.

'OK, everyone. Let's all stay cool!' the director called out loudly over the sound of excited chatter. 'I think this would be a good time to take a coffee break.'

'Has that ghastly woman finally lost her mind?' Neil asked. 'I always thought that she was a flaming nuisance—but I never realised that she was *totally* bonkers, as well! No wonder her ex-husband has been going around looking like a haunted man,' he added with a laugh. 'She's a real case of poison ivy!'

'Hmm…' Lois murmured, as puzzled as the rest of the company as to what had caused this extraordinary outburst.

However, following the arrival of the coffee trolley, and with no more repetition of the noise which had so abruptly halted the filming, most of the cast and crew soon resumed their places on set, ready to continue filming.

But it *really* wasn't the director's day. No sooner had he finally arranged matters to his satisfaction—a considerable delay having been caused by having to replace the broken arc lamp—than they were once again disturbed by the roar of a car, screeching to a halt in a shower of gravel, outside the front door.

'That's all I need!' the director groaned, as the front door was thrown open and a strange-looking man strode in amongst them.

For a moment there was a dead silence. Everyone stared mesmerised at the very tall, thin figure, whose long, straggly hair was dyed a bright green day-glo colour, and who appeared to be wearing an extraordinary outfit of black trousers and a high, wing-collared shirt beneath a long formal black frock coat reaching to his knees.

Gazing at the silky black top hat, swathed in a long black chiffon scarf, which was perched so rakishly on the green head, Lois was just thinking that the guy looked exactly like some crazy Victorian funeral attendant when Neil, standing beside her, gave a gasp of surprise.

'Good heavens!' he exclaimed excitedly. 'It's Frank N. Stein! What in the *hell* is he doing here?'

But before she could reply the identity of the man who was now standing in their midst also gradually dawned on the rest of the film crew. Ignoring the frantic calls of the director, they swarmed around the famous pop star, chattering away, congratulating him on his latest disc and asking for his autograph.

'Well—what it is to be famous!' Neil laughed, before moving swiftly across the room to join the excited throng.

'Have they all gone mad?' the director said as he walked over to Lois, shaking his head in puzzlement. 'The guy is only a singer, for heaven's sakes!'

'Ah—but he's a very rich and successful one,' Lois pointed out with a grin, staring over to where Martina's live-in lover was cheerfully signing the scripts of the actors, and whatever bits of paper the film crew could find.

She was just wondering whether Ace's ex-wife had been expecting the arrival of her boyfriend, when it became quite apparent that she had.

'There you are—at last!' she cried loudly, striding rapidly into the hall and brushing aside some of the crowd around the tall, thin man.

'What kept you so long?' she screeched, angrily gripping hold of his arm and dragging him firmly behind her as she stormed out of the hall. The sound of their footsteps could be heard thudding on the bare oak boards of the staircase, accompanied by the sound of Martina, still complaining loudly at the top of her voice.

'I wish I knew what was going on,' the director muttered, scratching his head in puzzlement. 'Still, I suppose we'd better try—yet again!—to see if we can't get this scene in the can.'

But he'd hardly begun to reassemble his crew once more when Joe Tucker and Martina returned to the hall, Joe carrying two bulging suitcases as he followed in his girlfriend's wake.

'I never, *ever* want to see this damn place again!' Martina yelled at the top of her voice, opening the front door to let Joe carry out the cases before turning dramatically around to face the astonished company.

'I hate and despise you all!' she continued in a high-pitched screech of anger. 'And how you can work with such a disgusting loose woman I've no idea!' she added, pointing a trembling finger towards the astonished figure of Lois. 'Just wait until I tell the newspapers all about what's been going on here—they'll have a field-day!' she added, giving another venomous shriek of shrill laughter before slamming the front door loudly behind her.

'Well—that's it! She's *definitely* flipped her lid,' Neil muttered, as Lois stood rooted to the spot beside him, totally stunned by the unexpected attack from Martina.

However, as she gradually began to pull herself together, she could feel a dark presentiment of trouble ahead slowly feathering down her spine.

Luckily, most of the crew had come to exactly the same conclusion as Neil Gray. Shrugging their shoulders and muttering amongst themselves, it appeared that they, too, thought that Martina must be in the midst of a highly hysterical nervous breakdown.

Calming everyone down, the director announced that, while he might be chancing his arm, he was going to have a third and final go at trying to film the scene. And they had, luckily, just finished the first fairly successful take, when there was yet another commotion. Because, rippling fast through the ranks of everyone in the room, and eventually reaching Lois herself, came the news that young Emily seemed to have completely disappeared.

'It's true,' Nora confirmed as she entered the hall, looking worried, a few moments later. 'I don't know where that dratted girl has got to—I'm sure I don't. Her father and I have been scouring every inch of this blessed house—and we can't seem to find her anywhere.'

'But...but I don't understand?' Lois gazed, stunned, at the older woman, her brain whirling after the events of the morning, when one extraordinary episode seemed to have followed another, almost at the speed of light. 'How do you know that Emily has disappeared? I mean...she could be anywhere in this house—or out in the park for that matter.'

Nora shook her head. 'No. Things have got a bit complicated, if you know what I mean.'

Lois shook her head in puzzlement. 'No, I *don't* know what you mean,' she told her, failing to understand why the elderly woman should be looking at her with such a heavy, significant expression on her face. 'Goodness knows what's been going on today, but Martina and her boyfriend have just stormed out of the house.'

'Well, she would, wouldn't she? Seeing how his nibs told her her fortune.' Nora chuckled. 'It seems that somehow Martina found out that you're expecting a baby. And she couldn't resist telling her ex-husband all about it. And why?' The old nanny gave a deep rumble of laughter. 'Because the stupid woman had got hold of an idea that he was sweet on you. Funny, that!'

'Oh, Lord!' Lois gasped.

'And that's not the half of it,' Nora informed her with a sly wink. 'When she tells his nibs that you're more than four months pregnant—and what's he doing, playing around with a loose woman?—he *doesn't* have hysterics and agree that he wouldn't touch you with a bargepole. Oh, no!' Nora grinned. '*He* just looks as pleased as punch and tells madam to ring up her boyfriend, pack her bags, and get out of the house as soon as maybe! So, what do you think about *that*?'

But Lois wasn't given any time to think about anything. While her mind was still trying to dizzily assimilate what Nora had said, she was startled to see Ace's tall figure striding across the hall towards her.

'I'm just off to try and track Emily down. I've got a good idea of where she may have got to,' he told Lois, looking tired and strained. 'I'll be back just as soon as I can,' he added, before quickly seizing her up in his arms and giving her a firm, resounding kiss, then letting her go and striding off out through the front door of the hall.

'Well! I never did!' Nora gasped beside her, clearly putting into words the various expressions on the faces of everyone in the hall as they stared at the pale face and trembling figure of Lois, clutching the mantelpiece for support as she desperately tried to cope with this fresh disaster.

CHAPTER EIGHT

'HAVE you heard any news…?' Lois asked anxiously as Nora popped her head around the door of the film star's private dressing room.

'It's all right. There's no need to worry, dearie,' the older woman told her with a beaming smile. 'His nibs seemed to have a good idea where Emily might have gone. And he finally tracked down the imp of mischief to where she was hiding—in that funny old Greek temple.'

'Thank God!' Lois breathed a heavy sigh of relief.

For everyone in the house, the past hour had been a very tense and worrying time. Over the last six weeks the actors and film crew had become very fond of Emily. Following her sudden disappearance, they'd huddled together in groups, trying to decide how best to help her father find the missing girl. However, the director had finally called them all together, before pointing out that there was little that they could do at the moment.

'It seems that Lord Ratcliffe has a good idea of where his daughter might be,' Peter Danvers had told them. 'But until he returns to the house—hopefully with his daughter in tow—I think we'll just have to keep calm, and be ready to offer our help if it should be needed.'

The director had also cancelled all work on the film set until such time as the situation became clearer.

Clearly worried about the pale-faced, agitated figure of the film's leading lady, he'd advised Lois that it might be a good idea for her to have a rest.

'Knowing Emily, I'm quite certain she'll turn up—

just like a bad penny!' he'd said, awkwardly placing a hand around her shoulders as the crowd of people gradually dispersed.

'I can't seem to…I can't seem to concentrate on anything at the moment,' she'd muttered helplessly.

'There really *isn't* anything any of us can do,' he'd told her firmly. 'If I was you, I'd get out of all that clobber you're wearing.' He grinned at the mad confection of feathers and ribbons piled up in her hair, over the extremely low-cut, lace-encrusted ivory satin costume. 'So, be a good girl and go and put your feet up, hmm?'

Lois had been touched by his kindly concern. 'I expect you're right,' she'd muttered, before trailing off to her own private dressing room, amidst the warren of small rooms at the back of the large house.

Entering the room which had once been the butler's 'Snug'—where, according to Ace, previous old butlers had spent their leisure hours, happily consuming their employer's best port and fine wines—she'd slowly followed the director's advice.

Having to wait for the assistance of Peggy Fraser before being able to remove her costume, Lois had sunk down onto the chair in front of the dressing table mirror; slowly removing the feathers, ribbons and sparkling jewels from her hair.

'Is Emily *really* all right?' Lois frowned anxiously up at Nora now, as she pulled out the last pin, releasing the long red curls, which tumbled down about her shoulders. 'I was so worried!'

The elderly woman nodded. 'We all were,' she confessed with a heavy sigh. 'What that poor girl has gone through, from first to last, doesn't bear thinking about.'

'But she really is OK?' Lois asked, quickly slipping

on a bandeau over her hair, before smearing heavy cream on her face.

'Oh, yes—she's as right as a trivet,' Nora assured her, as she lowered herself down into a comfortable armchair. 'Still a bit upset and tearful, of course. But then you'd expect that, wouldn't you? Especially with her stupid mother losing all control and shouting the house down.'

'But what I don't understand...' Lois muttered, as she began removing the heavy stage make-up required for filming beneath strong arc lights. 'I mean...why did she run away in the first place?'

Nora shrugged. 'I don't know all the ins and outs, dearie. But I expect she'll be able to tell you herself. The young imp is up in her bedroom—and I think she wants to see you, when you've got a minute.'

'*What?*' Lois spun around to stare at the elderly woman in startled surprise. 'Why on earth didn't you say so before now?' she cried, impatiently wiping the cream from her face, before jumping to her feet and dashing out of the room.

'Oh, Emily—*what* a fright you gave us all!' Lois said some moments later as she entered the teenager's bedroom. 'Are you all right? We were so worried about you.'

'I'm so sorry...' Emily told her, the tears streaming down her face as she sat huddled up on the edge of her bed. 'It's all my fault...everything is *always* my fault!' she burst out, before running across the room and throwing herself into Lois' arms.

Tightly hugging her thin, slight figure, Lois gently patted the girl's back until the storm of weeping gradually subsided.

'It's all right, kid,' she murmured, slowly leading Emily back across the room and sitting down on the bed beside her. 'You're back home now. Safe and sound. So there's no need to cry, OK?'

'But you don't…you just *don't* understand,' Emily hiccuped, gazing frantically around for something to stanch the tears still trickling down her cheeks. 'It's all my fault, you see.'

'I don't know what's wrong, but why don't you tell me all about it?' Lois murmured sympathetically, before going over to the girl's dressing table and returning with a large box of tissues.

'I reckon you've done enough weeping,' she said, handing the box to Emily. 'Come on. Dry your eyes— and spill the beans!'

The young girl nodded, gave her a weak, grateful smile as she grabbed a handful of tissues, wiping away her tears and loudly blowing her nose.

'I've been so stupid,' she confessed in a wobbly voice as Lois sat down once again beside her, putting a comforting arm about the thin shoulders. 'Dad's been really nice and kind, but even he thinks I've been a bit of an idiot,' she sniffed.

Lois shrugged. 'Look, kid—we've all done some damn silly things when we were much younger. That's all part of growing up. In fact, I'll bet that even your father—although he probably wouldn't like to admit it!—occasionally made a fool of himself when he was a young man,' she added with a grin. 'And, if it makes you feel any better, I still go hot and cold when I remember some of the really *awful* mistakes I made when I was your age.'

'You're being so kind—and I really don't deserve it,' Emily muttered, fiercely blowing her nose again. 'Because I broke my promise, you see. I promised that I wouldn't tell *anyone* about your baby. But…but…'

'But you told your mother…?' Lois murmured softly,

having by now had plenty of time to work out the probable sequence of events.

'Yes,' Emily whispered, covering her face as she began sobbing again.

'It's all right.' Lois gave her a comforting squeeze.
'After all, she *is* your mother. In fact, I reckon that I'd
no business putting such a burden on your young shoulders.'

The young girl shook her head. 'No...no, you don't
understand. We were having a really awful row, you
see,' Emily raised a tear-stained face towards her.

'Mummy kept going on *and on*...about how she
wanted to get back together with Dad. And she was being so foul and unkind about you.' The girl sniffed. 'I
mean...you've always been *so* nice to me. I know that
I wouldn't have a part in the film if you hadn't asked
the director to let me have a go. And...and when
Mummy kept yacking on and on, about how you were
the only person standing in her way...I blew my top!'
the girl admitted with another heavy sniff.

'We've all had rows with our parents. And, while it's
disturbing, it's really not the end of the world!' Lois
murmured, raising a hand to gently brush the girl's hair
from her brow.

'Yes, well...maybe I wouldn't have gone bananas if
I hadn't been so worried about Joe,' the girl confessed.
'Mummy just doesn't seem to care about him any more.
And so...when she said that you and Dad had a ''thing''
about each other—and if we didn't watch out, you would
soon be the new Lady Ratcliffe—I lost my temper and
told Mummy not to be so silly. That you were expecting
a baby, and so *of course* you couldn't be in love with
Dad! Not when you'd only met for the first time less
than six weeks ago.'

Oh, Lord! Lois thought, feeling quite sick and desperately trying to think what to do or say about the situation between Ace and herself.

It was terrifying to realise that she was ultimately responsible for so many problems. There was no way she could have known that her arrival here, at Ratcliffe Hall, would lead to such misery and unhappiness for so many people. However, it was clear that this awful mess—like some ancient Greek tragedy—had all been set in train right from the moment she'd first stepped over the threshold.

So, it was rapidly becoming clear to Lois that she must somehow try and sort out the problems she'd caused. Because she had no doubt that if some other actress had accepted the leading role in this film, Ace would still be calmly running his house and estate. While Emily—after spending a few weeks here with the film company—would have returned to school, and her normal way of life in London. But, most important of all, there would have been *no* reason for Martina—whose sharp female intuition and instinctive gut reaction about Ace and Lois had been quite correct—to have caused such a furore.

Lois knew that she must somehow try and put matters right. But exactly how she was going to do so she had absolutely no idea.

However, it was probably best to take one thing at a time. And clearly it was imperative to try and set this poor child's mind at rest.

'Now, look here, Emily,' she told the girl firmly. 'There's no way I'm blaming you for breaking your promise and telling your mother that I'm expecting a baby. Because you were, after all, only telling the truth.' She plucked a tissue from the box, gently wiping the girl's eyes. 'So, let's have no more tears, OK?'

'Thank you for being so nice,' Emily muttered. 'I only

ran away because…because I felt so ashamed of letting you down.'

'You didn't let *anyone* down,' Lois retorted quickly. 'So, put that idea right out of your mind straight away.'

Suddenly realising that Emily had probably run away from the house before Martina and Joe Tucker had made their spectacular departure, Lois saw that she could maybe offer the girl a more positive slant on life.

'I'm not sure what's going to happen in the future,' she said cautiously. 'However, I can tell you that Joe came down here this morning and collected your mother. So, I think there's a good chance that they've gone back to London. And I'm quite sure that your mother isn't…er…isn't thinking of coming back here, to Ratcliffe Hall, in the near future.'

'You mean…?'

Lois nodded. 'I don't know how things are going to turn out between them, of course,' she warned. 'But it looks as if there's a good chance your life could be returning to normal.'

'Do you really think so?' Emily asked hopefully, suddenly looking a lot more cheerful. 'But…but what about Dad? Mummy seemed *so* certain that he wanted her to come back and live here with him.'

'I really don't know what your father is intending to do,' Lois admitted, determined to keep the whole can of worms about the relationship between herself and Ace firmly off the agenda for the time being.

'I know it's hard on you, kid,' she added, fondly brushing her fingers through the girl's hair. 'All the same, I reckon you'll just have to leave the grown-ups to sort themselves out.'

Emily frowned. But before she could say any more the door opened and Ace strolled into the room.

'How are you, sweetheart?' he asked as he walked towards them. 'Are you feeling better now?'

Emily nodded. 'Yeah, I'm fine Dad,' she mumbled, hunching her thin shoulders and staring down at her nervously twisting hands in an agony of embarrassment. 'I've just been telling Lois that I'm really very…very sorry for causing so…so much trouble.'

While she'd been stammering out her apology Ace had turned to look over her bowed head at Lois, lifting one dark eyebrow in silent query. When she responded with a quick nod, indicating that Emily was basically all right, he looked visibly relieved.

'Well, I think we've all been sitting around feeling sorry for ourselves long enough,' he said firmly. 'Everyone is highly relieved that you're back home, safe and sound, Emily. So, as far as I'm concerned, that's the end of the matter. OK?'

'Yes.' Emily raised her face to give her father a slight, shamefaced grin. 'Thanks, Dad. I won't do it again.'

Ace laughed. 'I should damn well think not! Now, why don't you dry your tears, wash your face, and we'll see you downstairs at lunchtime?' he said, turning to put a hand on Lois' arm as she rose to her feet, before leading her out of the room.

'She's going to be fine,' Lois assured him as they walked down the corridor, Ace still maintaining a firm grip on her arm. 'I…er…I think I'll just go and get changed out of this dress,' she added nervously, finding herself almost running to keep up with his long stride.

Ace gave a snort of sardonic laughter. 'Oh, no—I don't think so!' he drawled, determinedly leading her past the door to her own bedroom.

'But I want to get out of this costume,' she protested breathlessly. 'It…it's very uncomfortable. And I haven't finished taking off my make-up, either.'

All of which was quite true, she told herself glumly, as he took not a blind bit of notice of what she was saying, but merely continued his rapid progress on down the small private staircase which led to his own suite of rooms.

Oh, Lord! There was no way she was up to coping with Ace. Not until she'd had the chance of some peace and quiet in which to work out just what she was going to do, following the dramatic events this morning. But it was becoming clear that he had no intention of letting her off the hook—even for five minutes.

A fact which he confirmed a few moments later, propelling her in front of him as they entered his large sitting room.

'It's *definitely* time you and I sorted out one or two items!' he drawled, firmly dragging her stiff, reluctant figure through a door at the far end of the sitting room, down a short passage, and into what was clearly his bedroom.

'Now, look here...' she began, determined to start this interview off on the right foot, fully in command of the situation. 'It's been a thoroughly disturbing morning for everyone. So I really think...'

Ace laughed. 'The trouble with you, Lois, is that you *think* far too much. What we need now is some straight *talking*!' And before she knew what was happening, he'd swept her up in his arms, striding swiftly over the thick carpet, before tossing her lightly down onto the large double bed.

'This is the only place where I can absolutely guarantee that we won't be disturbed,' he told her with a grin. 'There's no director around, to cry ''cut'' when you've had enough of the scene, either,' he added with a snort of caustic laughter, standing at the end of the bed

and gazing down at the girl who was glaring back up at
him.

'And it's no good scowling at me, Lois,' he continued
sternly, his firm tones belied by the sparkling amusement
in his gleaming grey eyes. 'Because you and I both know
that you've been a highly devious and *extremely* deceit-
ful woman!'

'I don't know what you mean,' she muttered helplessly, desperately wishing that she'd had some time to
prepare for this confrontation.

'When were you going to tell me?' he enquired
coolly. 'Of course, I can see it might have been just a
bit awkward to confess all right in the middle of filming.
So, perhaps you were intending to make a "grand announcement" at my supposedly secret fortieth birthday
party, hmm?'

Oh, God! This was clearly going to be *far* worse than
she'd imagined, she told herself with despair.

'Well?' Ace demanded, once again his stern voice and
expression sharply at variance with the warmth in his
eyes as he gazed down at the girl lying on his bed.

Still clothed in her gleaming ivory satin costume, with
its high waist and low-cut neckline amply displaying her
magnificent breasts, Lois was looking both totally ador-
able and fantastically sexy!

Unfortunately, as he'd now discovered, she also happened to be as clever as a cage full of monkeys! *And* as
slippery as an eel, Ace reminded himself sternly, struggling against an overpowering impulse to forget any
pressing questions or explanations—and simply gather
the lovely girl into his arms.

Forget it! he told himself grimly. You've got to get
this business sorted out, here and now. Otherwise, if you
don't watch out, this gorgeous creature is going to wrig-

gle and sweet-talk her way out of this house and back to America—taking your child with her!

'You've been here, at the Hall, for almost six weeks, Lois,' he told her sternly. 'So, why didn't you tell me?'

'Well...er...' Lois looked wildly around the room, seeking inspiration. Maybe he didn't *really* know? Not for certain... 'Well, the thing is, Nora asked us all to keep it a huge secret.'

Ace, who'd begun pacing restlessly about the room, suddenly stopped and turned on his heel to stare at her in bewilderment. 'What in the hell are you talking about?'

'Your birthday party, of course. Nora's gone to a great deal of trouble. She'll be devastated if she thinks that you've discovered her plans to give you a surprise birthday party.'

He stared at her blankly for a moment, and then threw back his head and roared with laughter. 'Oh, God— you're absolutely priceless, Lois, you really are!' he drawled sardonically, strolling back towards the end of the bed.

'OK...it was a good try,' he admitted, his broad shoulders still shaking with amusement. 'But as you know—only too well!—this conversation has absolutely *nothing* to do with Nora's surprise party. However, I'll definitely give you A for effort!' He gave another deep rumble of laughter. 'Now, do you think we can cut out all this nonsense and talk about the *real* reason why you're here? To put it bluntly: why didn't you tell me that you were expecting my child?'

'*Your child?*' she queried huskily, doing her best to look thoroughly shocked and startled. 'Where on earth did you get an idea like that?'

He frowned impatiently. 'Stop playing games with me, Lois! Surely you can't be trying to pretend that you're *not* pregnant? Because I understand from both my ex-wife and Emily that you're expecting a baby. I also hear that Nora and your dresser, Peggy Fraser, are in on the secret, too.'

As she gazed up at him in silence, he raked his hands irritably through his dark hair. 'Do I *have* to go and drag them both in here, just to prove the point?'

Lois shook her head. 'No, there's no need to do that,' she told him quietly. 'You're quite right. I am expecting a baby. But…but why should you think that it's anything to do with you?'

'Because I'm perfectly capable of counting up to ten!' he retorted. 'In this particular case, I understand that you are now four and a half months pregnant. And that, my darling Lois, is *precisely* and *exactly* the length of time since we made such wonderful love in the Philippines.

'And in any case,' he continued, as she opened her mouth, clearly prepared to continue the argument, 'I can very easily sort this matter out once and for all by the simple method of a blood test. You have heard of DNA, I presume?'

'*What*? No one's touching my baby!' she cried in alarm.

Ace sighed. 'You know very well that I'd never dream of doing such a thing,' he said, coming over to sit down on the bed beside her. 'Darling…surely you must see that this whole stupid argument is a complete waste of time?'

'Well…'

'Besides,' he murmured, placing a hand gently on her stomach, 'I *know* that's my child in there.'

The total certainty in his voice struck a chill into her heart. However, with a supreme effort, Lois made one last, spirited attempt to stand her corner.

'Look, you're a lovely guy. And I'll freely admit that I find you devastatingly attractive, but...'

'Believe me—it's entirely mutual!' he murmured, lowering his head to give her a long, loving kiss.

'For heaven's sake!' Lois protested huskily as he slowly released her, struggling to pull her scattered wits together.

'But...but, the thing is,' she continued breathlessly, 'we only had what might be referred to as *one* "night of passion", all those months ago.' She gave him a brief, wintry smile. 'So, it's really a bit much for you to now claim this child as your own, isn't it?

'After all,' she went on as he remained silent, 'you know absolutely nothing about my life. I might well have a long-term, live-in boyfriend back in the States, who could easily be the father of this child.'

He shook his head, his lips tightening ominously. 'Rubbish! I refuse to believe that you're the sort of woman who, while involved in a serious relationship, would go so far as to make mad, passionate love to any Tom, Dick or Harry whom she met on holiday.'

'Of course I'm not like that!' she retorted quickly, before feeling sick as she realised that she'd neatly fallen into his trap.

Because Ace was quite right. If she'd had a long-term lover, she really *wasn't* the sort of woman to fall breathlessly into another man's arms.

'OK—you win,' she muttered helplessly. 'Yes, I guess I'll have to agree that you are the father of this child I'm expecting. But that doesn't give you any rights as far as its future is concerned.'

'"Any rights"...?' he echoed blankly, before rising swiftly to his feet and pacing angrily about the room. 'Don't be so damn stupid, Lois! That's *my* son or daughter you're carrying,' he exploded as he turned around to face her. 'And I'm not going to stand one more minute of this nonsense. Quite clearly, the first thing we must do is to get married. I can see no problem about arranging a special licence, and I know the local vicar would be only too pleased to...'

Lois lay back on the pillows, gazing at the man she loved so much as he walked briskly back and forth across the room. Ticking off the various items on his fingers, he was clearly far too busily absorbed making arrangements for their future life together to give any thought to *her*.

It was just as though he was going through a shopping list, she told herself grimly. But he'd never said that he truly loved her, had he? All he seemed concerned about at the moment was claiming her baby as his child, and getting married as soon as possible.

And then, like a dash of cold water, she suddenly realised what lay behind this whole business. She had no problem in recalling Emily's words on her first evening here at Ratcliffe Hall. '...of course, what Dad really *needs* is a son.' When she'd questioned the girl further, Emily—clearly amazed by Lois' total ignorance concerning the laws of English aristocratic inheritance—had retorted, 'To inherit the title, of course!'

So, she now clearly understood why Ace—the louse!—was so desperately keen to get married as soon as possible. Well...to hell with him!

'I suppose you're hoping for a son?' she murmured acidly, as Ace stopped pacing and approached the bed. 'To inherit the title?'

He shrugged. 'Well, yes...I suppose so. To be honest, I hadn't really thought about it.'

'Oh, yeah?' She snorted with derision. 'Well, dream on, buddy! If you want a son and heir—you're going to have to marry someone else. Because I'm simply not interested in applying for the job!'

'What on earth are you talking about?' He stared down at her in puzzlement, disturbed by the sharp, caustic note in her voice.

Lois gave a shrill, high-pitched laugh. 'You *may* be able to prove that the baby I'm expecting is yours. But there's no law on this earth that can make me marry a man who doesn't truly love me,' she told him grimly, struggling to sit up and swing her legs off the bed. 'As far as I'm concerned,' she added, 'you can take a hike!'

'*What...?* Are you seriously trying to tell me that you're refusing to marry me just because you think I don't love you?'

'Got it in one!' she snapped. 'What's more, I'm not interested in your title—for either myself or my baby. So, we're both going back to America as soon as possible. And there's damn all you can do about it!' she added angrily, although most of her fury was directed against herself, for having been such an idiot as to fall for this rotten man.

'Don't be so bloody stupid!' Ace growled, his tall figure stiff with anger as he pushed her back down on the bed once more. 'You must know that I'm absolutely *crazy* about you! God knows, I haven't thought about anyone—or anything—since I first set eyes on you!'

But by now Lois had the bit firmly between her teeth, and she wasn't prepared to listen to anything he might say.

'Get lost!' she grated bitterly. 'Of course you're expressing your undying love *now*. But it's just too damn late, isn't it?'

'For God's sake!' he bellowed angrily. 'How can you be such a blithering idiot?'

'Oh, I'm an *idiot*, am I?' she snapped, her temper by

now well out of control. 'Well, I'm quite *sane* enough to know that you only want to marry me because I come as a package deal—baby included! And I'm not so desperate to have a wedding ring on my finger that I'd be prepared to marry a man who didn't love me. For your information there are *plenty* of really good-looking sexy guys back home in America who... *Hey*! Leave me alone!' she yelled, struggling to escape from beneath the strong hands now pressing her firmly down onto the mattress.

As she glared up at the man leaning over her, Lois saw that there was now a hard, sensual cast to his hawk-like features; her stomach knotted in sudden tension as his fingers moved slowly and erotically over her breasts, almost fully exposed by the low-cut gown.

'Cut it out, Ace!' she muttered, suddenly breathless as his head came slowly down towards her; her nostrils were filled with his musky scent, every fibre of her being trembling violently as his mouth followed his hands, which had now slipped inside the bodice of her costume, releasing her firm breasts. As his lips closed over the hard, swollen tips, taut and aching for his touch, she moaned helplessly, shivers of excitement rippling through her body at the sensual heat of his lips and tongue caressing her bare flesh.

'This...this is *not* the answer!' she gasped as he slowly raised his head to stare down at her. 'And...and I'm not going to change my mind, either!' she cried, rolling violently away and scrambling off the bed.

'So...OK...I'll freely admit that you're a real tiger in the sack, Ace,' she told him bitterly, her cheeks flushing as she frantically pulled up the bodice of her gown to cover her nakedness. 'But there are a lot of things more important than...than sex!'

'Oh, really?' he drawled, reclining at ease against the

pillows and regarding her with an enigmatic expression on his face. 'Such as...?'

Lois tried desperately to clear her mind, her body aching and throbbing with unsatisfied need and desire.

'Well, such as...um...such as... *Oh, hell*! I'm not sticking around here to have a long, philosophical discussion about basic human morality!' she yelled at him angrily. 'I'm not marrying you—and that's *that*!' she added fiercely, before swiftly gathering up her long skirts and dashing towards the door.

'Oh, yes—you will!' he called out after her, the sound of his harshly sardonic, mirthless laughter echoing in her ears as she ran for the safety of her own room.

The next two days were ones which Lois would have preferred to forget.

She'd seen virtually nothing of Ace. Not that she believed he'd completely abandoned any attempt to marry her. He wanted an heir too badly to do that. However, she had far more pressing and immediate issues to deal with. Such as having to put the director and producer of the film fully in the picture.

Worried about any negative publicity which Martina might stir up, she'd had a long, private conversation with the two men. They had both known she was pregnant, of course. But now she knew that she'd have to level up and confess that Ace was the father of her baby.

'Phew! That's a turn-up for the books,' Dave Green, the producer had muttered, while Peter Danvers had just looked down at his feet, obviously embarrassed by the whole scenario.

'I'm sorry to put you in this mess, boys,' she said with a heavy sigh. 'I can give you my solemn promise that neither Lord Ratcliffe or myself had *any* idea we'd be meeting up like this. In fact, I nearly died with shock on arriving here to discover that he owned this stately home,' she confessed with an unhappy laugh. 'Believe me—it's been a nightmare!'

Clearly, both men were dying to ask the obvious question: if she was expecting his baby—how come Lois hadn't even known the man's name, or where he lived? But, equally clearly, they were both far too well-mannered to dream of raising the awkward subject.

It was just as well that she was dealing with two excessively polite, uptight Englishmen! Lois told herself, struggling to control a hysterical bubble of grim laughter, before swiftly putting them in the picture about the danger of Ace's ex-wife talking to the newspapers.

'I don't think there's any need to worry,' Dave Green told her. 'There's only three more days of filming to go. Right, Peter?' When the director nodded, Dave added, 'Sol Weiser is thrilled with the some of the rushes flown out to him last week. So, I reckon he's not going to pull the financial rug and abandon this film now. Not when it looks like being a success.

'As for that awful woman, Martina—I suggest we forget her,' he continued. 'Even if she *does* go to the papers with a story about you and Lord Ratcliffe, they aren't going to print anything potentially libellous. Certainly not until they've checked with our PR unit. And I see no problem in stalling any journalists—for the next few days at least.'

'Dave's right,' the director agreed, pointing out that when the news did break—which it was bound to, once her pregnancy became too obvious to hide—it was likely to be only a nine-day wonder. 'There's no reason why it should damage either the film or your career,' he told her comfortingly.

'In fact, it could be really good for the film's publicity!' the producer chimed in enthusiastically. 'I can just see the headlines now...'

'Thank you, Dave!' She grimaced. 'I think I'd rather *not* think about it just at the moment—if you don't mind?'

'Oops—sorry!' He'd grinned, before promising that both he and the director wouldn't say a word to any of the film crew about the paternity of her child.

Unfortunately, and goodness knows how, the 'word' clearly *had* seeped out. Not that anyone was unkind, or made any malicious remarks. In fact, now that it seemed to be common knowledge amongst the film crew that she was expecting a baby, Lois had been touched by just how supportive everyone was being.

She was also aware of the fact that many of the film crew seemed to have a very good, accurate idea of exactly *who* had fathered her child.

It had undoubtedly been the sight of Ace, crushing her in his arms and planting a firm kiss on her lips—in full view of everyone on set—before going off to look for his missing daughter, which had fuelled their suspicions. And, unlike the young teenager, Emily, they'd obviously had no problem in working out the likely scenario: she and Ace must have become involved with one another long before the filming had started at Ratcliffe Hall.

All of which had done nothing to relieve the depression, which seemed to be bearing down heavily on her shoulders.

It wasn't too bad when she was working, of course. Being surrounded by so many people, and having to concentrate on both remembering her lines and acting a part, meant that she had very little time to think about her own, personal problems. But when filming ceased and the cameras were packed away for the day, there was little to soothe her inner torment.

If Ace had at any time, before that tempestuous confrontation in his bedroom, made any mention of the fact that he loved her, it would be a different matter. But how could she trust a man who'd vowed that he did, in fact, care deeply for her only *after* he'd discovered that she was carrying his child—a possible heir to Ratcliffe Hall? She was prepared to do a lot for her unborn baby. But marry a man who didn't *truly* love her...? No way!

'It's no good you trying to persuade me, either,' she'd told Nora, who'd clearly been told by Ace to try and twist her arm. 'He doesn't really care for me, you know. All that rotten guy is interested in is having a son to inherit his title.'

'Don't be so daft!' Nora snorted. 'I've known him, man and boy, all his life. So I know what I'm talking about when I say that I've *never* seen anyone so crazy about a woman—not in my whole life!

'Besides,' the elderly woman added firmly, 'I knew he was head over heels in love with you long before any of this nonsense started. It was as plain as the nose on my face!'

Lois shrugged. 'If it was so plain, it's amazing how he never actually managed to get around to saying anything, isn't it?'

'Well, you can't have it both ways, dearie.' The old nanny shrugged. 'As I understand it, you made the poor fellow promise to keep his hands off you until the end of the film. Well, that didn't give him much chance to tell you how he felt, did it?' she added as Lois remained obstinately silent.

'I'd say that you just lost your temper with His Lordship,' Nora continued shrewdly. 'And you said a lot of things which you now wish you hadn't. But you're stiff with pride, and not prepared to admit that you're even slightly in the wrong. In fact, if you ask *me*, I think it's time somebody banged some sense into that beautiful head of yours, dearie!'

'Well, nobody *is* asking you, are they?' Lois snapped, marching out of the room and slamming the door loudly behind her.

But she'd only taken a few steps down the corridor before she felt sick with remorse. How *could* she have been so rude and aggressive towards Nora? Especially when the elderly nanny had shown her nothing but kindness, and been so sweet and helpful when she'd fainted in the middle of the film set.

Quickly retracing her steps, she entered the housekeeper's room, taking a deep breath before apologising for having behaved so badly.

Nora had forgiven her with a warm smile. 'All the same, dearie,' she'd pointed out quietly, 'Your life would be so much easier if you *could* bring yourself to acknowledge the truth. Because I'm pretty sure that all you *really* want is for His Lordship to seize you up in his arms and carry you off into the sunset—just like they do in all those lovely romantic novels.'

'Oh, Nora—real life isn't like that,' Lois had murmured sadly. 'In fact, I reckon that real life is mostly a total pain in the neck!'

'You've got a point there.' The elderly woman had given a deep rumble of laughter. 'However, if you take my advice, you'll try and think of a way to get down off that high horse of yours. And no,' she'd added quickly, 'I'm not mentioning this conversation to His Lordship. I reckon this is something that you two are going to have to sort out for yourselves.'

Walking slowly back to her room, Lois had been forced to agree that Nora had a point. It *was* her own stupid pride which was standing in the way of her happiness. But she and Ace weren't the only people involved, were they? There were so many other factors to which he didn't seem to have given any thought at all.

What about Emily, for instance?

She hadn't seen much of the young girl, since most mornings had been taken up with filming the 'below stairs' scenes. However, she had no idea how Emily would react to the baby. And with such a very difficult, unpredictable mother, there was no saying what would happen if Lois and Ace did get married. For instance, Martina might well try and prevent Emily from paying any visits to her father. Lois certainly didn't want to be responsible for the subsequent unhappiness which such a decision would inevitably cause.

Most important of all—there was the question of what she was going to do about Ace...

Lois was prepared to admit, if only secretly to herself, that Nora had been quite right. Of course the rotten man was crazy about her. Just about as crazy as she was about him! But all the same...there was no denying the fact that Ace also wanted an heir, to inherit both Ratcliffe Hall and its ten thousand acres.

But...*and this was the sixty-four-thousand-dollar question*...would he have asked her to marry him if she hadn't been expecting his baby?

To be absolutely honest, Lois still had severe doubts on that score. In fact, she was by no means certain that he would have done anything of the sort.

CHAPTER NINE

THERE was an old joke in the film business. Question: What does a film star have to do to earn a million pounds? Answer: Just stand around all day doing nothing!

Lois smiled grimly as she recalled the old gag. Few people outside the film industry seemed to have any idea of the long, tedious hours spent by actors waiting, fully costumed and made-up, while various alterations were made to the set. And this afternoon's session was no different.

Dressed once again in her ivory-coloured gown, Lois had been waiting, with the other actors, with mounting impatience, to shoot again the scene which had been so rudely interrupted by Martina's abrupt departure from Ratcliffe Hall.

However, it was the very last scene to be filmed in the huge old stately home, and perhaps that was why the director seemed to be taking so much time before calling everyone in front of the cameras. Because this would be his last chance to film the scene, before the actors and film crew scattered to the four corners of the world first thing tomorrow morning.

Lois gave a heavy sigh. The past six weeks had, without a doubt, been the most traumatic of her whole life. Packing her suitcases earlier this morning, she'd been feeling desperately tired and deeply depressed. So, in a strange way, it would prove to be a relief to escape from the unhappy and miserable situation in which she found herself—even if it meant leaving behind the man she had come to love so very dearly.

If only she could sort out the tangled muddle in her mind! Unfortunately, there seemed so many questions which needed answering. And her confrontation with Ace, late last night, had done nothing to really clarify the situation.

Much earlier in the day, she'd bidden a fond farewell to Emily, who was being driven back to London by her father. Carefully avoiding Ace's eyes as he stood beside his large, black Mercedes—waiting while his daughter said goodbye to her friends amongst the actors and film crew—Lois had given the young girl a big hug.

'I will see you again, soon, won't I?' Emily had said anxiously, as her father impatiently called for her to get into the car. 'Mummy and Joe seem to be getting on all right now. And, actually…' she'd grinned up at Lois '…I'm quite looking forward to going back to school and seeing all my old friends.'

'Well, just make sure you're nicer to your teachers in future!' Lois had told her with a laugh, surprised to realise just how much she was going to miss the young girl. In fact, she'd felt quite a lump in her throat as she'd stood at the front door, watching the big black car disappear off down the drive.

However, it could only be good news to hear, however much she might have disliked the woman, that Martina had so swiftly cut her losses as far as her ex-husband and Ratcliffe Hall were concerned. And with any luck she and Joe Tucker would, once again, settle down happily together.

It was not a view shared by Ace. As he'd told her forcefully, on his return later that evening, 'I can't see that relationship holding out for much longer!'

Perhaps it had been a mistake to ask whether Emily

was all right when she'd unexpectedly bumped into him in that long, dark corridor following his return from London late last night. She'd only been concerned about the young girl's welfare, of course. But Ace had clearly had other things on his mind.

'I can't see that young man Tucker putting up with much more of Martina's nonsense. But then, who knows why two people should find themselves insanely drawn to one another?' he'd murmured as she'd backed nervously away from his tall, broad-shouldered figure.

He didn't move as he stood before her, effectively blocking her escape. But all at once the atmosphere in the dark corridor seemed to become filled with an aura of menace, and highly charged sexual tension. Her mouth suddenly felt dry and parched, her pulse almost racing out of control as she was swept by an overpowering, totally mad urge to throw herself into his arms. A crazy impulse—which she swiftly and ruthlessly crushed without mercy.

'I must…I really must go and finish my packing,' she muttered, glancing nervously about her for a route of escape.

'Must you, really…?' he drawled sardonically as she decided to brazen it out, defiantly raising her chin as she prepared to walk past him towards the stairs. 'I can think of a better way to spend your time.'

His rapid movement gave her no time to escape. One moment, it seemed, there had been the width of the corridor between them. And then, a heartbeat later, she found herself a prisoner in his arms, her breasts being cruelly crushed against his hard, firm chest. Instinctively trying to avoid his embrace, she threw herself backwards, the force of her action bringing her spine into jarring contact with the wall behind. Desperately wriggling and twisting to free herself, Lois realised from the darkening gleam in his hooded grey eyes, and the sudden hardening of the thighs now pressing her so closely to the wall, that her struggles and writhing body were merely increasing his excitement and arousal.

'Leave…leave me alone, Ace!' she demanded huskily.

'Don't be so damned stupid!' he retorted grimly. 'How can I leave you alone? You are my first thought when I wake in the morning—and the last before I go to sleep at night. For heaven's sake, woman! I'm desperately in love with you. So, asking me to leave you alone is a totally impossible request. It…well, it's like asking the Niagara Falls to start flowing backwards! It can't be done.'

She shook her head wearily. 'That's just lust. I'm not saying that it's not a powerful force,' she added hurriedly, 'but it keeps clouding the issues between us. You don't seem to realise that there are so many problems…so many questions which need answering.'

Ace stood still, staring down intently at her for some moments.

'Very well,' he said with a heavy sigh, finally breaking the strained silence. 'It's probably a waste of time, but I want you to give me one last opportunity to try and knock some sense into that lovely head of yours. And no,' he added, with a snort of grim, caustic laughter, 'I won't lay a finger on you. OK?'

'Well…all right,' she muttered, convinced she was making a bad mistake as he propelled her stiff, reluctant figure down the stairs to his sitting room.

'I could do with a stiff drink. But maybe in your condition…?' he said a few moments later, handing her a soft drink before carrying his own whisky over to a large, comfortable chair some feet away from where she was sitting on a nearby sofa.

'As far as I'm concerned, Lois, the situation is very simple,' he said, lowering himself down into the chair and slowly taking a sip from his glass. 'I fell madly in love with you over four months ago, and my feelings haven't changed since then. In fact, incredible as it may seem—especially in the light of recent dramatic events!—they have grown deeper and more intense.

'Which is not surprising, I suppose,' he added with a shrug. 'After all, we are both adults, and we know that one night of passion—however wonderful it may have been—is not enough on which to build a lasting relationship.'

Lois silently nodded her head. Totally abandoning his usual air of warm, relaxed charm, Ace was now presenting a side of himself which she hadn't seen before. In fact, the ultra-cool, businesslike assessment of his emotions by the man sitting opposite her was proving to be considerably daunting.

'I'm quite old enough to know the difference between lust and love,' he told her. 'And, since I *am* in love with you, it seems perfectly reasonable that I should want us to get married. The fact that you are carrying my child merely makes it necessary to bring the date of our wedding nearer than we might have originally planned. But I can assure you, my darling,' he added with a brief, wintry smile, 'I would still want to marry you—and would happily do so tomorrow—even if you *weren't* expecting a baby.

'In fact, you *must* know that any suggestion of wanting to marry you because of some ''package deal'' that includes your baby is *utterly* and *totally* absurd!'

'Yes, well...' Lois muttered, her cheeks flushing with embarrassment. 'OK...I'll admit I went a bit overboard there. I guess I sort of lost my temper, and said a lot of stupid things...'

Ace waved a dismissive hand. 'We were both at fault,' he shrugged. 'However, having thought long and hard about this problem,' he continued, 'the only solution that I can see, to put your mind at rest about any devious motives I might have, is to suggest that we don't get married until *after* the child is born. That would ensure, if you give me a son, that he will definitely be unable to inherit the title. Of course, if it's a boy, he might not thank you for mucking up his inheritance!' Ace added with a grim snort of laughter. ,''However, I'm not worried about that. Because all I'm interested in is having you for my wife. And spending the rest of my days together with you here at Ratcliffe Hall.'

Stunned by the huge sacrifice he was clearly prepared to make, on her behalf, Lois slowly put down her glass on the table beside her.

'I...I really don't know what to say,' she began slowly. 'However, such plain speaking and...and generosity, demands that I'm equally honest with you, Ace. So, yes, I *do* care deeply for you. But...even if we leave aside the baby, and its possible inheritance, I have to say that I still have so many other doubts and problems on my mind. Such as the question of Emily, for instance,' she added, explaining her fears about the reaction of the girl herself, and the very probable trouble which could be caused by Martina.

'And then there's the question of my career.' Lois shrugged her slim shoulders. 'I've been an actress for the past ten years. And it's been damned hard work at times—especially trying to climb the greasy pole amidst all the in-fighting among Hollywood executives. However, now I've got to the top of my profession, I'm not sure I want to throw it all up. I mean...winning that Oscar last year made me a very bankable proposition. Which, in turn, means I can earn a helluva lot of money.

So,' she added with another shrug, 'I can't just chuck my whole career down the pan—not without a good deal of thought.'

'Yes, I do see…'

'Hang on a minute—I haven't finished! You can have your say in a minute,' she told him, a brief smile taking the sting from her words.

'OK…' she continued as he gave her a brief nod. 'Another subject we haven't touched on is this huge old house. As far as I can see, it's a bottomless pit as far as finance is concerned—right?'

He laughed. 'That's probably putting it a bit strongly. However, I'll agree that it requires a great deal of money to be spent on its restoration. I'll also freely admit that running the place doesn't come cheap.'

'That's just what I reckoned.' She nodded. 'The trouble is…I don't know how much money you've got. Especially since all you aristocratic Englishmen go around in old tweeds which wouldn't look out of place in a cheapo second-hand shop. Which is why,' she added, over his rumbling of amused laughter, 'I'd be a fool not to think hard and long about taking on both you and the massive financial responsibility of Ratcliffe Hall.

'I don't want you to get the wrong idea,' she told him hurriedly. 'I mean, I'd hate you to think I was tough and calculating. But I've been in far too many hard, fierce bargaining situations with my agent—making sure I got properly paid by the film companies—to suddenly lose all financial sense now.'

'Fair enough,' he agreed with a grin. 'Especially as I've always wanted to marry a rich woman who'd keep me in the lap of luxury!'

'OK…OK! You can cut out the wisecracks—because I know that you're not pushed for a few dollars,' she retorted. 'But doing up this old pile is going to take a *real* fortune. I'm not saying I couldn't afford it—because I can—but if I've got to underwrite the whole bang-shoot, I'd be an idiot not to think hard and long about giving you my bank book as well as my hand and my heart. Right?'

'Absolutely right,' he agreed. 'And we'll come back to that point in a minute. However, to answer some of your earlier points, particularly about Emily, I can tell you that she's absolutely thrilled about the idea of us getting married.'

'You mean…?'

'Yes, we had a long talk in the car, on the way back to London. The poor girl was obviously worried about the situation between Martina and Joe Tucker, so I assured her that she'd always be welcome to spend her holidays here. And that since I hoped to be able to persuade you to marry me, it would be a lot more fun for her to visit a proper family home—rather than just a collection of huge empty rooms lived in by a grumpy old father. All of which, naturally, led to my confession that we *had* met earlier this year, and that—'

'*Oh, no*! You didn't really…?'

'Yes, of course I did,' he retorted quickly. 'Emily isn't a fool. As I told her, I was paying her the compliment of recognising that she was quite old enough to know that grown-ups could make mistakes, and that accidents could happen. However, I emphasised the fact that I'd been completely and utterly bowled over from the first moment I met you. And that I desperately wanted to have both you and our child living here with me at the Hall.'

'And she wasn't upset?'

Ace grinned and shook his head. 'No. In fact, to quote my dear daughter's words on the subject: "I think that sounds really cool, Dad—absolutely wicked!"' His eyes twinkled with amusement. 'In fact, Emily has asked me to send you her best love. She thinks it's a "whizzo" idea for us to get married—and would you please try to concentrate on giving birth to a girl, since she's always wanted a sister.'

Startled by the removal of so many of her fears and worries about Emily's likely reaction to his plans, Lois couldn't think what to say. By the time she'd marshalled her thoughts, Ace was already dealing with the other points she'd raised.

'As far as your career is concerned, I wouldn't dream of standing in your way,' he assured her earnestly, since he could well appreciate that, having striven so hard, she might be loath to throw away all her hard work. 'Although I would be happier if you cut down on your workload, spending more time here, with myself and our children.

'Now, as far as this house is concerned,' he continued, 'I'm very touched that you might have been prepared— after due thought, of course!—to undertake its restoration. However, my dearest one, I must tell you that although I may go around looking as though I buy my clothes at an Oxfam shop...' he chuckled '...I am, in fact, a very wealthy man. There seemed no point in spending a fortune on doing up this place merely to house a single, divorced man. However, with the prospect of it becoming a warm and happy family home, I'd have no problem in being able to pay the bills to bring it back to its former glory.'

There was a long silence while she considered what he'd said.

'I know you feel that I've been rushing you, Lois, making arrangements for the marriage and so on. But I've been only too well aware that time is against us.' He sighed. 'Tomorrow is the last day of filming and then you're off to America—or wherever. Which is why I've felt it's so important that we get everything sorted out as soon as possible.

'I hope that I've answered all your problems and worries.' He gave a helpless shrug of his broad shoulders. 'I can only say: whatever happens between us, I know there will never be another woman for me. And, if I was to be truly honest, I'm desolated by the thought of losing you.'

'Oh, Ace…!' she moaned, tears springing to her eyes at the warmth and tenderness in his voice. 'I'm in such a muddle…I honestly don't know what to do…'

'It's all right, my darling,' he murmured, coming swiftly across the room to sit down beside her and enfolding her in his arms. 'There is just *one* more item…and I don't know how I had the strength not to mention it before now…but you know that I'm just crazy about you—and can't keep my hands off your delicious body,' he breathed thickly, lowering his mouth to brush and tantalise her trembling lips, his hands moving slowly over her silk gown, sensually caressing her soft curves.

He was right, she realised with despair. They really *were* so good together. Which was why she always found it so difficult to keep a clear head whenever he was anywhere near her.

'No! Please…please, Ace—you've got to listen to me!' she muttered, desperately trying to push him away. 'I…I know that we've got this terribly strong attraction between us. And…and that's mostly the trouble, you see. Because I can't seem to think straight nowadays. Not when you're sitting so close to me, as you are now,' she confessed with a tearful smile. 'And besides, getting married is such a big step. And…and I'm terrified of making a mistake—just like my parents. I can remember all the deep unhappiness, and guilt, because I felt that it was all *my* fault they were breaking up. And although I know it's stupid, and I had nothing to do with the breakdown of their marriage, I'm still so worried, and...'

'Ah! Now it seems that we've come to the nub of the problem, right?'

She nodded. 'Yes, it's taken me a long time to work out why I was so frightened, in the past, of getting too involved with anyone. And...and why I'm so afraid of now taking what seems such a very, *very* large step.'

'But, my darling—if we truly love each other, and I believe that we do, that love *will* be enough to carry us through.'

She slowly and sorrowfully shook her head. 'I still can't really make up my mind what to do for the best. I honestly need more time...' She rose to her feet. 'I'm sorry, Ace. I love you as much as I'm capable of loving anyone,' she added, walking slowly towards the door. 'The trouble is, I just don't know if it's enough.'

'You may not know *your* own mind,' he told her, remaining sitting on the sofa as she slowly opened the door. 'But I certainly know *mine*! So, it looks as if I'll have to do something about the situation, doesn't it?'

All the long night, and throughout today, while she wasn't actually acting in a scene, Lois had been running his words through her mind. There had been nothing in either the tone of his voice or the words themselves which had been threatening. But, all the same, she'd been aware of a cold, hard determination lying behind what he'd said.

However, Lois knew that she was right. It would be quite wrong to take such an important decision without really thinking it through. For her, marriage meant a lifelong union. And, with the rising number of so many unhappy divorced parents nowadays, she was desperately anxious to make sure that she didn't rush blindly into marriage—however attractive the prospect might be. So, she'd leave tomorrow morning. Perhaps when she was well away from Ace, and Ratcliffe Hall, she'd be able to put everything into its proper perspective. In any case...

'OK. We're all ready now. Everyone on set, please,' the director called out, his order cutting through her thoughts.

With a sigh, she lifted her long skirt and began making her way towards the large marble mantelpiece to resume filming the final scene of *Lady Susan*.

Ace had made an accurate guess about the surprise birthday party which had been planned for him by Nora. However, he was clearly taken aback to be called onto the set—just as the final scene had been shot—to find himself facing a truly enormous iced cake, covered in forty candles.

He was surrounded by everyone still dressed in their costumes, and a glass of champagne was quickly pressed into his hands. Then came the heartfelt cry from a young sound recordist: 'Hurry up and cut the cake, mate. We're all starving!'

Laughing, Ace did as he was bid. And then, as the noise level rose in direct relation to the amount of champagne being consumed, there were increasingly clamorous loud calls of: 'Speech... Speech!'

Slowly putting down his glass, Ace grinned, allowing himself to be persuaded to mount a large wooden box.

'Well, first of all, I must thank everyone for what has turned out to be a real surprise,' he admitted, amidst the sounds of laughter.

'I knew Nora would be planning something—but I'd assumed that she was going to produce this cake at dinner, tonight. However,' he added, reaching down for his glass and holding it up in front of them, 'I would like to thank you all for what has, quite frankly, been one of the most enjoyable six weeks of my life. I'm sure your film deserves to be a real success—and I wish you all the very best of luck!'

There was a general round of applause, with even one or two of the younger members of the crew bursting into a verse of 'For he's a Jolly Good Fellow', before Ace held up his hand for silence.

'I said that it's been one of the most enjoyable times of my life—but actually, I think I was understating the case. Because you see before you a very, *very* happy man. No one likes to feel that they're getting any older. But what does turning forty matter, when I've been so fortunate—at one and the same time—to find the woman of my dreams?

'Yes—I can see that you've guessed our secret,' he continued, amidst the sound of clapping and laughter. 'I'm afraid that the good lady and I have…er…slightly anticipated our wedding vows.' He grinned at the increasingly ribald gales of laughter. 'But now I can assure you that I'm aiming to rectify the situation—and we will be getting married as soon as possible!

'And so, ladies and gentlemen, I would ask you to raise your glasses to the woman who is about to make me the happiest of men—Miss Lois Shelton!'

As Lois stood turned to stone, totally stunned by this rapid turn of events, one of the young cameramen, obviously a director in the making, quickly turned one of the large spotlights onto her trembling figure.

'I definitely am *not*…it's all a *dreadful* mistake!' she wailed as Peggy and Nora laughingly pushed her for-

ward, towards Ace, who quickly bent down and pulled
her up on the box beside him.

'Are you out of your mind?' she demanded angrily.

'Shush!' he cautioned with a grin. 'Remember your
public, darling. Give them a big smile, there's a good
girl!'

'I'll kill you for this! she hissed savagely out of the
side of her mouth as Ace, clearly playing to the audience, gallantly raised her hand to his lips.

'You know that I've *no* intention of marrying
you...you foul man!' she added grimly, while trying to
keep a warm smile firmly fixed on her face.

'That's what *you* think!' he laughed, before clasping
her tightly in his arms and kissing her soundly, his action
increasing the laughter, cat-calls and whistles of the as-
sembled company.

When he finally released her, Ace informed her, beneath the noise surrounding them, 'I've already got hold
of a special licence. I've booked the church and, you'll
be glad to hear, my dearest one, I have also sent the
formal announcement of our wedding to the newspapers.
So, I don't really see how you can back out now, do
you?' He laughed, before turning back to wave at their
audience.

'That's what *you* think!' She mimicked him in a low,
furious voice, only her years of training as an actress
enabling her to keep a stiff, forced smile on her lips in
response to the many cries of 'Good luck,' and, 'Health
and Happiness to you both,' which resounded around the
large hall.

'I refuse to be blackmailed like this, Ace,' she told
him in a fierce undertone. 'And I definitely *won't* marry
you—not now—*not ever*!'

CHAPTER TEN

BUT of course she *had* married him! Ace told himself, recalling the past with a grin as he gazed across the crowded hall to where his adored wife was sitting, warm and comfortable beside the fire.

It had been a hell of a struggle to get his beautiful Lois to the altar—but he'd managed it, at last! And here they were, eight months later, even happier and more in love than on the day when they'd married, a week after the film crew had left Ratcliffe Hall.

My God—he was a lucky man! And *doubly* blessed, too, he reminded himself, as Lois gazed tenderly down at his small son, held securely within her arms. Unable to repress a broad smile, he watched as she turned to say something to Emily—sitting beside her on the comfortable sofa and holding his new baby daughter as if she was handling a delicate piece of glass.

He was still having great difficulty in getting used to the idea that he was now the father of twins. Who'd have thought it? Although he would never have any problem remembering the date of their birthday—arriving, as they had, on a cold and crisp Christmas morning three months ago!

Nora was, of course, totally over the moon at having *two* babies to look after. And she had been much involved, together with Emily, in planning this large party after the christening, and in trying to decide what names to give the children.

Ace had got his own way about his daughter by simply stating that she was to be called Eloise—and refusing to discuss the matter any further. He'd also—thankfully!—managed to firmly squash Nora's mad idea that his young son should be named after himself.

'Algernon...? Are you out of your tiny mind?' he'd thundered incredulously, before insisting that Lois should make the decision.

And when, without a moment's hesitation, she'd put forward the name of his dead brother, Mark, Ace had known exactly *why* he'd fallen so desperately in love with such a warm, kind and totally wonderful woman.

'Hey, man—this is a really cool christening party!' an American exclaimed, giving Ace a friendly slap on the back while helping himself to another glass of champagne from the tray of a passing waiter. 'And I'm really mad about this huge, crazy old house. Way to go!'

Having absolutely no idea who this extraordinarily good-looking young American might be, Ace merely smiled in agreement, before leading the unknown guest towards where Peggy Fraser and the director, Peter Danvers, were chatting quietly together.

'You're so square, Dad, that you're positively cubic!' Emily had said earlier in the day, just as they were all about to go to church for the christening. 'But take it from me that *all* Lois' friends from America are going to be drop-dead famous film stars or directors. And I'll *die* if you put your foot in it! So, *please* try and be cool.'

Mindful of his daughter's strict instructions, Ace now drawled smoothly, 'I'm quite sure, Peggy, that I don't have to introduce this gentleman to you...?'

'I should think not!' Peggy giggled, before turning to the tall, good-looking American. 'I just *loved* your last film, Brad. It's been a smash hit, here in England, and I can't wait to hear about the one you're making at the moment.'

Having done his duty, Ace quickly scanned the room,

checking that everyone's glasses were full to overflowing, before moving over to sit down on the arm of the sofa beside his wife.

'You're looking a little tired. Are you sure this isn't all too much for you?' he murmured quietly.

'No, darling—I'm fine,' Lois told him, smiling lovingly up into his gleaming grey eyes, her nerve-ends tingling as he slipped a hand beneath her curly red hair, gently massaging the back of her neck.

The twins' birth had not been an easy one, and she knew just how off-putting Ace had found that fact, carefully striving to restrain his ardour when they had resumed their lovemaking. But she was now feeling a great deal stronger, and was aware that her body was becoming eager and impatient to welcome the full force of his passion.

They were so lucky, she told herself gratefully, both in having two wonderful young babies and in the way that Emily had greeted their marriage with such enthusiasm. In fact, there had been no holding Emily back from insisting on becoming a godmother to small Eloise.

'After all, she is *my* sister,' the teenager had announced proudly, clearly feeling far more settled now that her mother and Joe Tucker had followed Lois and Ace's example by getting married.

And what a christening it was turning out to be! Ace had insisted on choosing the date—a year to the very day from when they'd first met in the Philippines. He really was amazingly romantic, for an Englishman! But then, maybe all the national barriers were fading away, she thought, gazing around at the extraordinary mix of many world-famous film stars and a large cross-section of the local gentry—who all seemed to be getting on like a house on fire.

'Well, now...Lady Ratcliffe!' one of her old

Hollywood girlfriends said with a grin. 'I saw that film you made in this house at a showing in Los Angeles, just the other day. I reckon it's going to be a smash hit! So, what are your future plans? Any films in the pipeline?'

'Well…' Lois gazed up at her husband, whose tall figure had suddenly become very still, at the careful, guarded expression on his handsome face. Darling Ace clearly feared the worst. But he really had no need to worry, because she'd had plenty of time to sort out her priorities.

'I've given the matter a great deal of thought,' she said, turning back to her friend, 'and finally come to the conclusion that it's time I retired.'

'But…but you simply *can't* do that!' The other woman gazed at her in dismay. 'Not after you won that Oscar. Why, you can just about name your price—for any production.'

'I really am far too busy at the moment,' she murmured, grinning as she caught the low, muffled sound of her dearest husband's deep sigh of relief.

'Oh—come on, honey! Even I've heard all about English nannies, for heaven's sake. And since you've decided to settle down here, in England, it couldn't be easier to…'

'No, I've made up my mind,' Lois told her firmly. 'I'm not knocking Hollywood, or the film business, because I've had great fun for a number of years. But I was offered—and have accepted—a far more interesting and important role.'

'Oh, wow! You mean that you're *actually* going to join the Royal Shakespeare Company…at Stratford-upon-Avon…?' Her friend gasped in amazement.

Lois laughed and shook her head. 'No, of course not—you idiot! I was referring to my new, truly marvellous, permanent role…that of Lord Ratcliffe's leading lady!'

'And let's not forget our "package deal"', Ace reminded Lois with a grin.

'What *deal*?' the actress muttered, clearly confused as husband and wife dissolved with laughter.

'Oh, didn't Lois tell you that I was *desperate* for a son and heir…?' Ace drawled, his deep voice heavy with amusement. 'So, when I discovered she was pregnant, I had to force myself—with the *greatest* reluctance, of course!—to ask her to marry me. In fact, I only agreed to wed my darling wife because, as she so clearly pointed out, she came as a "package deal"—with baby included!'

He shook his dark head in mock sorrow. 'Unfortunately, something seems to have gone dramatically wrong with the scenario. Because we've now got *two* babies, and…'

But the rest of his words were lost beneath the sound of Emily's spirited protest as he gathered her stepmother and their new baby son into his arms, before firmly possessing his wife's lips in a warm, tender kiss of total love and commitment.

'*Get real, Dad*! We all know that you're crazy about Lois. And I think she's really, *really* wicked, too!'

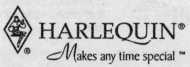

Not The Same Old Story!

Exciting, glamorous romance stories that take readers around the world.

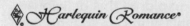

Sparkling, fresh and tender love stories that bring you pure romance.

Bold and adventurous—Temptation is strong women, bad boys, great sex!

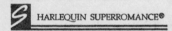

Provocative and realistic stories that celebrate life and love.

Contemporary fairy tales—where anything is possible and where dreams come true.

Heart-stopping, suspenseful adventures that combine the best of romance and mystery.

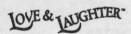

Humorous and romantic stories that capture the lighter side of love.

**Race to the altar—
Maxie, Darcy and Polly are**

in a fabulous new
Harlequin Presents® miniseries by

LYNNE GRAHAM

These three women have each been left a share of
their late godmother's estate—but only if they marry
withing a year and remain married for six months....

Maxie's story: **Married to a Mistress**
Harlequin Presents #2001, January 1999

Darcy's story: **The Vengeful Husband**
Harlequin Presents #2007, February 1999

Polly's story: **Contract Baby**
Harlequin Presents #2013, March 1999

Will they get to the altar in time?

Available in January, February and March 1999
wherever Harlequin books are sold.

EXPECTING

She's sexy, she's successful... and she's pregnant!

Relax and enjoy these new stories about spirited women and gorgeous men, whose passion results in pregnancies... sometimes unexpectedly! All the new parents-to-be will discover that the business of making babies brings with it the most special love of all....

Harlequin Presents® brings you one **EXPECTING!** book each month throughout 1999.
Look out for:

The Baby Secret by Helen Brooks
Harlequin Presents #2004, January 1999

Expectant Mistress by Sara Wood
Harlequin Presents #2010, February 1999

Dante's Twins by Catherine Spencer
Harlequin Presents #2016, March 1999

Available at your favorite retail outlet.

HARLEQUIN®
Makes any time special ™

Look us up on-line at: http://www.romance.net   HPEXP1

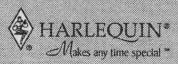

Coming Next Month

HARLEQUIN PRESENTS®

THE BEST HAS JUST GOTTEN BETTER!